"I'm not safe here. Seth isn't safe here. We have to go."

"Where will you go that you'll be safe?"

"I..." Addie blew out a breath, tears filling her eyes, and if this hadn't been so serious, he would have up and walked away. He didn't do tears.

But this was too big. Too important.

"I don't know," she whispered, one of the tears falling over her cheek.

Noah had the oddest urge to reach out and brush it away. "Then you'll stay."

"Noah."

"If you don't know where to be safe, then you'll stay here, where people are ready and willing to protect you and Seth."

"I can't put any of you in this, Noah. It's dangerous."

"Not if you tell us what we're up against." Not that it'd change his mind. He'd fight a whole damn army to keep her here.

"Promise me you'll stay." And they were a little too close, standing here like this, and even as Seth bounced in her arms and reached for his hat, their eyes didn't leave each other.

WYOMING COWBOY PROTECTION

NICOLE HELM

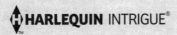

HARLEQUIN INTRIGUE®

To my husband, who always asks, "Do you need time to write?"

ISBN-13: 978-1-335-63954-7

Wyoming Cowboy Protection

Copyright © 2018 by Nicole Helm

Recycling programs
for this product may
not exist in your area.

Printed in U.S.A.

HARLEQUIN®
www.Harlequin.com

Nicole Helm grew up with her nose in a book and the dream of one day becoming a writer. Luckily, after a few failed career choices, she gets to follow that dream—writing down-to-earth contemporary romance and romantic suspense. From farmers to cowboys, Midwest to *the* West, Nicole writes stories about people finding themselves and finding love in the process. She lives in Missouri with her husband and two sons and dreams of someday owning a barn.

Books by Nicole Helm

Harlequin Intrigue

Carsons & Delaneys

Wyoming Cowboy Justice
Wyoming Cowboy Protection

Stone Cold Texas Ranger
Stone Cold Undercover Agent
Stone Cold Christmas Ranger

Harlequin Superromance

A Farmers' Market Story

All I Have
All I Am

Falling for the New Guy
Too Friendly to Date
Too Close to Resist

Visit the Author Profile page at Harlequin.com.

CAST OF CHARACTERS

Noah Carson—A taciturn rancher who wants nothing to do with his new housekeeper or her baby, but when both are in danger, Noah will do anything to keep them safe.

Addie Foster—On the run from her sister's murderous ex, Addie will do anything to keep her nephew safe, even pretend he's her son. She takes a job as Noah's housekeeper in isolated Bent, Wyoming, hoping no one will find them.

Seth Foster—Addie's nephew, not quite one year old. Most people think Seth is Addie's son.

Peter Monaghan—Mob boss from Boston. Peter has been chasing Addie across the country. He'll stop at nothing to get his son back and hurt Addie for stealing him away.

Laurel Delaney—A distant relative of Addie and a sheriff's deputy in Bent County. Laurel gets Addie the job with Noah, then helps keep her safe from Peter.

Grady Delaney—Noah's cousin owns a bar in Bent. He's engaged to Laurel. When Peter shows up in Bent, Grady helps Noah keep Addie and Seth safe.

Ty Carson—A former army ranger and Noah's brother, Ty helps Noah keep Addie safe.

Vanessa Carson—Noah's cousin, who helps Addie and Seth stay safe.

Chapter One

August

Addie Foster watched from the car's passenger seat as a whole new world passed by her window. If she'd thought Jackson Hole was like nothing she'd ever known, Bent, Wyoming, was an alien planet.

She'd grown up in the heart of Boston, a city dweller always. Occasionally her family had traveled up to Maine for quaint weekends or vacations in little villages, enjoying beaches and ice-cream shops.

This was not that. This wasn't even like those dusty old Westerns her grandpa had loved to watch as he'd reminisced about his childhood being a Delaney in Bent, Wyoming—as if that had ever meant anything to Addie.

It meant something now. Seth fussed in his

carrier in the back seat and Addie swallowed at the lump in her throat. Her sister had died trying to protect this sweet little man, and Addie had spent the past nine months struggling to protect him.

The baby's father hadn't made it easy. Addie had been able to hide Seth for three months before Peter Monaghan the 5th had discovered her sister's deception, and *no one* deceived Peter Monaghan the 5th.

For six months, Addie had crisscrossed her way around the country, running out of false identities and money. Until she'd had to call upon the only person she could think to call upon.

Laurel Delaney.

Addie had met Laurel at Addie's grandpa's funeral some twenty years ago. They'd taken an instant liking to each other and become pen pals for a while.

They'd drifted apart, as pen pals always did, once the girls got into high school, and Addie never would have dreamed of calling Laurel out of the blue until desperation led her to think of the most faraway, safe place she could imagine. Someplace Peter would have no reach. Someplace she and Seth would be safe from his evil crime boss of a father.

"Don't worry," Laurel said pleasantly from the driver's seat as Seth began to cry in earnest. "We're only about five minutes away. I'm sorry I can't have you stay with me, but my place is pretty cramped as it is, and Noah needs the help."

Noah Carson. Addie didn't know anything about him except he was some relative of Laurel's boyfriend, and he needed a housekeeper. Addie didn't have experience keeping anyone's house, let alone a ranch, but she needed a job and someplace to stay, and Laurel had provided her with both. In the kind of town Peter would never dream of finding on a map, let alone stepping foot into.

She hoped.

"I'm going to have to apologize about Noah, though," Laurel said, maneuvering her car onto a gravel road off the main highway. "This is kind of a surprise for him."

"A surprise?" Addie repeated, reaching into the back and stroking her finger over Seth's leg in an effort to soothe.

"It's just, Noah *needs* the help, but doesn't want to *admit* he needs the help, so we're forcing his hand a bit."

Addie's horror must have shown on her face, because Laurel reached over and gave

Addie's arm a squeeze, her gaze quickly returning to the road.

"It's fine. I promise."

"I don't want to be in anyone's way or a burden, Laurel. That isn't why I called you."

"I know, and in an ideal world Noah would hire you of his own volition, but we don't live in an ideal world. Noah's cousin, who used to do most of the housekeeping, moved out. Grady—that's Noah's other cousin—tried running an ad but Noah refused to see anyone. This, he can't refuse."

"Why?"

Laurel flicked a glance Addie's way as she pulled in front of a ramshackle, if roomy-looking, ranch house.

"Addie, I know you're in trouble."

Addie sucked in a breath. "You do?"

"I could be reading things wrong, but I'm guessing Seth's father isn't a very good man, and you need to get away from him."

Addie swallowed. It was the truth. It wouldn't be a lie to tell Laurel she was right. Seth's father was a terrible man, and Addie desperately needed to get away from him.

"I'm a cop, Addie. I've dealt with a lot of domestics. This is the perfect place to get away from a guy who can't control himself. You're safe here. In Bent. At the Carson Ranch, and with me looking out for you." Laurel smiled reassuringly.

"I just…" Addie inhaled and exhaled, looking at the house in front of her. It looked downright historical. "I need a fresh start. I'd hate to think it's built on someone who doesn't want me around."

"Noah might not want you around, but he needs you around. The way I see it, you two need each other. Noah might be quiet or gruff, but he's not a jerk. He'll treat you right no matter how much he doesn't want you to be here. I can promise you that."

"And the baby?"

"I've never seen Noah hurt anyone, and I've known him all my life and worked in law enforcement here for almost ten years. But most especially, I've never seen him be cruel to anyone, even Delaneys. He's not an easy man to read, but he's a good man. I'd bet my life on that."

The door to the house opened and a big, broad, bearded man stepped out. He wore jeans and a T-shirt, the lines of a tattoo visible at the sleeve. His grin was like sin, and all for Laurel. So this couldn't be the quiet, reserved Noah she was apparently ambushing.

"That's your man?" Addie asked, watching him saunter toward where they were parked. She'd never seen two people just look at each other and flash sparks.

Laurel grinned. "Yes, it is. Come on. Let's get you introduced."

NOAH GLOWERED OUT the window. Damn Grady. More, damn Laurel Delaney getting her Delaney nose all up in his Carson business. Since he wasn't the one sleeping with her, Noah didn't know why he had to be the one saddled with her relative.

But saddled he was.

The young woman who got out of the passenger seat looked nothing like a housekeeper, not that a housekeeper had ever graced the uneven halls of the Carson Ranch. He came from hardscrabble stock who'd never seen much luxury in life. Never seen much purpose for it, either.

Noah *still* didn't, but all his help had moved out. Grady was off living with a Delaney. Vanessa, who'd once taken on much of the cleaning and cooking responsibilities—no matter how poorly—had moved into town. His brother, Ty, came and went as he pleased, spending much of his time in town. Any time he spent at the ranch was with the horses or pushing Noah's buttons. Noah's teenage step-cousin was as helpful as a skunk.

Noah was running a small cattle ranch on his own, and yes, cleaning and cooking definitely fell by the wayside.

Didn't mean he needed an outsider lurking in the corners dusting or whatnot. Especially some wispy, timid blonde.

The blonde pulled a baby out of the back seat of the car. And she had a baby no less. Not even a very big-looking baby. The kind of tiny, drooly thing that would only serve to make him feel big and clumsy.

Noah's scowl deepened. He didn't know what to do with babies. Or wispy blondes. Or people in general. If only the horses could housekeep. He'd be set.

The door opened, Laurel striding in first. Noah didn't bother to soften his scowl and she rolled her eyes at him.

Noah was a firm believer in history, and the history of Bent, Wyoming, was that Carsons and Delaneys hated each other, and anytime they didn't, only bad things came of it. Noah didn't know what Laurel had done to Grady to change Grady's mind on the importance of the feud, but here they were, ruining his life. As a couple.

It was a shame he liked Laurel. Made all his scowling and disapproval hard to hang on to.

The blonde carrying the baby stepped in behind Laurel, followed by Grady.

"Noah," Laurel said with one of those smiles that were a clear and sad attempt to get him to smile back.

He didn't.

"Noah Carson, this is your new house-keeper, Addie Foster, and her son, Seth. Addie, this is Noah. Ignore the gruff Wyoming cowboy exterior. He's a teddy bear underneath."

Noah grunted and Grady laughed. "Ease up there, princess. No one's going to believe that."

Laurel shot Grady a disapproving look. "The point is, Noah will be a fair and, if not pleasant, a *kind* employer. Won't you, Noah?"

He grunted again. Then looked at the blonde. "Thought you were a Delaney."

"Oh, well." Addie smiled, or tried to. "Sort of. My grandfather was one." She waved a nervous hand, her eyes darting all around and not settling on any one thing.

"I'll show you to your room, and Noah and

Grady can bring in the baby stuff," Laurel said cheerfully, already leading Addie and baby down the hall like she owned the place.

"Come on, let's get the stuff," Grady said once the women were gone.

"Remember when this was my house because I was the only one willing to work the ranch full time?" Noah glanced back at where the two women had disappeared. "Your woman's going to get baby ideas," he muttered.

Grady scoffed, but Noah noted that he didn't argue.

Which was to be expected, Noah supposed, but Noah hated change. Especially uncomfortable change. People change.

"You don't have to be prickly about it. You're going to have a clean house and a few home-cooked meals. Try a thank-you."

"You know me a lot better than that," Noah returned as they opened the trunk to Laurel's car.

Grady sighed, grabbing a stroller. "Laurel thinks Addie's in a bit of trouble."

"What kind of trouble?"

"Laurel's theory? Abusive husband."

"Hell," Noah grumbled. He didn't know what to do with babies, and he definitely didn't know what to do with a fragile woman who'd been the victim of abuse.

"She just needs a fresh start is all. Somewhere she feels safe. I'll keep an eye out for any other jobs that'll work while she's got the baby, but this is important. And it isn't like you don't need the help."

"It isn't that bad."

Grady looked at him dolefully as they hefted a menagerie of baby things out of Laurel's trunk and headed toward the house. "Pretty sure you were wearing that shirt yesterday, cousin."

Noah looked down at the faded flannel work shirt. "No, I wasn't." Maybe. He didn't mind doing laundry, but he hated folding laundry, and then the clean and dirty sometimes got a little mixed up if they weren't muck clothes.

Grady stepped inside, but Noah paused on the stairs. He looked back over his shoulder at the mountains in the distance. Clouds were beginning to form and roll, and there'd be a hell of a storm coming for them soon enough.

On a sigh, Noah stepped inside. This was his idea of a nightmare, but he wasn't a jerk who couldn't put his own wants and preferences on the back burner for someone in trouble. If the woman and the baby were really running from some no-good piece-of-trash ex...

He'd suck it up. He might be growly and taciturn, but he wasn't a bad guy. Not when it came to things like this. She might be related to a Delaney, but he knew what violence could do to a family. Carsons couldn't help but know that, and he'd promised himself he wouldn't be like them.

Somehow it had worked out. This generation of Carsons wasn't half as bad as the last, if a little wild, but he and Grady and Ty stood up for people who couldn't stand up for themselves. He wouldn't stop now.

Even if the woman and her baby did have Delaney in their blood.

Noah walked down the hall and into the room where Grady was already setting up all the baby gear for Addie while Laurel cooed over the baby in her arms. Noah gave Grady a pointed look but Grady ignored it.

"Well, we better get going and let you have some settle-in time," Laurel said, looking around the room as if inspecting it. "You can call me day or night. Whatever you need, or Seth needs."

"Thanks," Addie said, and Noah tried not

to frown over the tears shimmering in the woman's eyes. Hell, female tears were the worst thing. Laurel and Addie hugged, the baby between them, before Grady and Laurel left. Laurel paused in front of Noah.

"Thank you," she mouthed, holding a hand over her heart.

Noah merely scowled, but the annoying thing about Laurel was she was never fooled by things like that. She seemed to be under the impression he was the nicest one of the lot.

Noah hated that she was right.

"So, I'll leave you to settle in," Noah offered, not expressly making eye contact considering this was a bedroom. "Need anything, let me know."

"Oh, but... Shouldn't I be saying that to you? I mean, shouldn't we go over duties? Since Laurel and Grady set this up, I... I'm not sure what you expect of me." She bounced the baby on her hip, but Noah figured it was more nerves than trying to keep the boy from fussing.

He tried to smile, though even if he'd accomplished it he knew it was hard to see beyond the beard. "We can do it in the morning."

She blinked at him, all wide blue-eyed innocence. "I'd like to do it now. This is a job, and I should be working it."

"It's Sunday. Rule number one, you don't work on Sunday."

"What do I do then?"

"I don't care, but I'll cook my own meals and clean up after myself on Sundays. Understood?"

She nodded. "What's rule number two?"

Timid. He did not know what to do with timid, but he was being forced. Well, maybe he needed to treat her like a skittish horse. Horse training wasn't his expertise, but he understood enough about the animals to know they needed a clear leader, routine and the opportunity to build their confidence.

Noah glanced at the hopeful young woman and tried not to grimace.

"I have a checklist," she blurted.

"A checklist?"

"Yes, of duties. Of things I do for people. When I'm housekeeping. I… You…"

The sinking feeling that had been plaguing him since Grady announced his and Laurel's little plan that morning sank deeper. "You haven't done this before, have you?"

"Oh." She looked everywhere around the room except him. "Um. Well. Sort of."

"Sort of?"

"I… I can cook, and clean. I just haven't ever been on a ranch, or lived in someone else's house as their employee. So that's, um, well, it's super weird." She glanced at the kid in her arms. "And I have a baby. Which is weird."

"Super weird," he intoned.

She blinked up at him, some of that anxiety softening in her features. "If you tell me what you want me to do, I promise I can do it. I'm just not sure what you expect. Or want."

"I'll make you up a checklist."

She opened her mouth, then closed it, then opened it again. "I'm sorry, was that a joke? I can't exactly tell."

Noah's mouth twitched of its own accord. "Settle in. Get the baby settled in. Tomorrow morning, six a.m., kitchen table. We'll discuss your duties then."

"Okay."

He turned to go, but she stopped him with a hesitant "um."

He looked over his shoulder at her.

"It's just, could you give us something of a tour? A map? Smoke signals to the bathroom?"

Noah was very bad at controlling his facial

features, half of why he kept a beard, so the distaste must have been clear all over his face.

"I'm sorry, I make jokes when I'm nervous."

"Funny, I just shut up."

Those big blue eyes blinked at him, not quite in horror, but not necessarily in understanding, either.

"Sorry," he muttered. "That was a joke. I joke when I'm nervous, too."

"Really?"

"No. Never," he replied, chastising himself for being prickly, and then ignoring his own chastisement. "Follow me. I'll show you around."

Chapter Two

September

Addie liked to use Seth's afternoon nap for laundry folding and listening to an audiobook, then dinner prep. She'd been at the Carson Ranch for a full month now, and while she couldn't claim comfort or the belief she was truly safe and settled, she'd developed a routine, and that was nice.

She found she liked housekeeping, much to her surprise. As an administrative assistant in the family business—a franchise of furniture stores Grandpa had moved to Boston to run when his father-in-law had died suddenly back in the fifties—she'd hated waiting on people, keeping things and meetings organized. She'd taken the job because it had been expected of her, and she hadn't known what else to do with her life.

So, the fact keeping everything neat and organized at Noah's house, making meals and helping the ranch run smoothly felt good was a surprise. Maybe it was the six months of being on the run and not having a house or anything to care for except Seth's safety.

Maybe it was simply that she felt, if not safe here, like she *fit* here.

Addie worked on chopping vegetables for a salad, the baby monitor she'd bought with her first overly generous paycheck sitting on the sill of the window overlooking the vast Carson Ranch. She hadn't needed a monitor in any of the previous places she'd been. They were all hotel rooms or little one-room apartments where she could hear Seth no matter where she went.

Now she had a whole house to roam, and so did Seth. They had these beautiful views to take in. For as long as it lasted, this life was *good*.

Some little voice in the back of her head warned her not to get too attached or settle in too deeply. Peter could always find her here, although it was unlikely. She hadn't shared anything with her father since he'd cut off Kelly long before Seth, and she'd been on shaky ground for *not* cutting Kelly off as well.

As for the rest of her friends and family, she'd sent a cheery email to them saying she'd gotten an amazing job teaching English in China and she'd send them contact information when she was settled.

If anyone had been suspicious, she'd been long gone before she could see evidence of it.

Addie didn't miss Boston or her cold father or even the furniture store that was supposed to be her legacy. That was also a surprise. Boston and her family had always been home, though not exactly a warm one after Mom had died when Addie'd been a kid. Still, striking out and starting over as a faux single mom had been surprisingly fulfilling. If she discounted the terror and constant running.

But she wasn't running right now. More and more, she was thinking of the Carson Ranch as *home*.

"You are a hopeless idiot, Addie Foster," she muttered to herself.

She startled as the door swung open, the knife she'd been using clattering to the cutting board from nerveless fingers.

But it was only Noah who swept in, looking as he always did, like some mythical man from a Wild West time machine. Dirty old cowboy hat, scuffed and beaten-up cowboy boots. The jeans and heavy coat were modern enough, but Noah's beard wasn't like all the fashionable hipster ones she was used to. No, Noah's beard was something of an old-fashioned shield.

She found herself pondering a little too deeply what he might be shielding himself from. Snapping herself out of that wonder, she picked up the knife. "You're early," she offered, trying to sound cheerful. "Dinner isn't ready yet."

It was another thing she'd surprisingly settled into with ease. They all three ate dinner together. Noah wasn't exactly a talkative guy, but he listened. Sometimes he even entertained Seth while she cleaned up dinner.

He grunted, as he was so often wont to do, and slid his coat and hat off before hanging them on the pegs. She watched it all through her peripheral vision, forcing herself not to linger on the outline of his muscles in the thermal shirt he wore.

Yes, Noah had muscles, and they were not for her to ogle. Though she did on occasion. She was *human*, after all.

"Just need to call the vet," he said.

"Is something wrong?"

"Horses aren't right. Will there be enough for dinner if Ty comes over?"

"Of course." Addie had gotten used to random Carsons showing up at the house at any time of day or night, or for any meal. She always made a little extra for dinner, as leftovers could easily be made into a lunch the next day.

Gotten used to. She smiled to herself as Noah grabbed the phone and punched in a number. It was almost unfathomable to have gotten used to a new life and think she might be able to stay in it.

Noah spoke in low tones to the vet and Addie worked on adding more lettuce to the salad so there would be enough for Ty. She watched out the window at the fading twilight. The days were getting shorter and colder. It was early fall yet, but the threat of snow seemed to be in the air.

She loved it here. She couldn't deny it. The mountains in the distance, the ramshackle stables and barns. The animals she didn't trust to approach but loved to watch. The way the sun gilded everything gold in the mornings and fiery red in the evenings. The air, so clear and different from anything she'd ever known before.

She felt at *home* here. More so than any point in her life. Maybe it was the circumstances, everything she was running from, how much she'd taken for granted before her sister had gotten mixed up with a mob boss. But she felt it, no matter how hard she tried to fight it.

She could easily see Seth growing up in this amazing place with Noah as something like a role model. Oh, it almost hurt to think of. It was a pipe dream. She couldn't allow herself to believe Peter could never find them here. Could she?

Noah stopped talking and set the phone back in its cradle, looking far too grim. Addie's stomach clenched. "Is everything okay?"

"Vet said it sounded like horses got into something chemical. Poison even," Noah said gruffly with no preamble.

Any warmth or comfort or *love* of this place drained out of Addie in an instant. "Poison," she repeated in a whisper.

Noah frowned at her, then softened that imperceptible amount she was beginning to recognize. "Carsons have some enemies in Bent. It isn't unheard of."

It was certainly possible. The Carsons were a rough-and-tumble bunch. Noah's brother,

Ty, could be gruff and abrasive when he was irritated. Grady was certainly charming, but he ran a bar and though she'd never spent any time there since the ranch and Seth took up most of her time, Laurel often spoke disparagingly of the clientele there.

Then there was Noah's cousin Vanessa. Sharp, antagonistic Vanessa would likely have some enemies. Or Grady's troublemaking stepbrother.

The problem was none of them lived at the ranch full-time. They came and went. Noah could be grumpy, but she truly couldn't imagine him having enemies.

She, on the other hand, had a very real enemy.

"Are you sure?" she asked tentatively.

"Look, I know you've had some trouble in your past, but who would poison my horses to get at you?"

He had a point. A good point, even if he didn't know the whole story. Peter would want her and Seth, not Noah or his horses. He'd never do something so small and piddly that wouldn't hurt *her* directly.

"Trust me," Noah said, dialing a new number into the phone. "This doesn't have a thing to do with you, and the vet said if he gets over here soon and Ty helps out, we'll be able to save them." Noah turned away from her and started talking into the phone, presumably to his brother, without even a hi.

Addie stared hard at her salad preparations, willing her heart to steady, willing herself to believe Noah's words. What *would* poisoned horses have to do with her?

Nothing. Absolutely nothing. She had to believe that, but everything that had felt like settling in and comfort and routine earlier now curdled in her gut.

Don't ever get too used to this place. It's not yours, and it never will be.

She'd do well to remember it.

October

NOAH FROWNED AT the fence. Someone had hacked it to pieces, and now half his herd was wandering the damn mountains as a winter storm threatened in the west.

He immediately thought of last month and the surprise poison a few of his horses had ingested. The vet had saved the horses, but Noah and Ty had never found the culprits. Noah liked to blame Laurel and her precious sheriff's department for the crime still being unsolved, even though it wasn't fair.

Whoever had poisoned the horses had done a well enough job being sneaky, but not in creating much damage. For all he knew it was some kids playing a dumb prank, or even an accident.

This right here was no accident. It was strange. Maybe it could be chalked up to a teenage prank, but something about all this felt wrong, like an itch he couldn't reach.

But he had to fix the fence and get the cows before he could worry about wrong gut feelings. Noah mounted his horse and headed for the cabin. He'd have to start carrying his cell to call for help if these little problems kept cropping up.

What would Addie be up to? She'd been his housekeeper for two months now, and he had to admit in the quiet of his own mind, he'd gotten used to her presence. So used to it, he relied on it. She kept the cabin neat and clean, her cooking was better and better, and she and the boy… Well, he didn't mind them underfoot as much as he'd thought he was going to.

Maybe, just maybe, he'd been a little lonely in that house by himself earlier in the summer, and maybe, just maybe, he appreciated some company. Because Addie didn't intrude on his silence or poke at him for more. The boy was loud, and getting increasingly mobile, which sometimes meant he was crawling all over Noah if he tried to sit down, but that wasn't the kind of intrusion that bothered him. He found he rather enjoyed the child's drooly smiles and screeches of delight.

"What has happened to you?" he muttered to himself. He looked at the gray sky. A winter storm had been threatening for days, but it hadn't let down its wrath yet. Noah had no doubt it would choose the most inopportune time possible. As in, right now with his cows scattered this way and that.

He urged his horse to go a little faster. He'd need Grady and Ty, or Vanessa and Ty if Grady couldn't get away from the bar. Maybe even Clint could come over after school, assuming he'd gone today. This was an all-hands-on-deck situation.

But as he approached the cabin, he frowned at a set of footprints in the faint dusting of snow that had fallen this morning. The footprints didn't go from where visitors usually parked to the door, but instead followed the fence line before clearly hopping the fence, then went up to the front window.

A hot bolt of rage went through Noah. Someone had been at that window watching Addie. He jumped from the horse and rushed into the house. Only when he flung open the door and stormed inside did he realize how stupid he looked.

Addie jumped a foot at her seat on the couch, where she was folding clothes. "What's wrong? What happened?" she asked, clutching one of his shirts to her chest. It was an odd thing to see, her delicate hands holding the fabric of something he wore on his body.

He shook that thought away and focused on thinking clearly. On being calm. He didn't want to scare her. "Somebody broke the fence and the cows got out."

Addie stared at him, blue eyes wide, the color draining from her dainty face as it had the day of the poisoning. He'd assured her *that* had nothing to do with her, and he believed it. He believed this had nothing to do with her, too, but those footsteps and her reaction to anything wrong or sudden…

He wondered about that. She never spoke of Seth's father or what she might be fleeing, and her actions always seemed to back up Laurel's theory about being on the run from an abusive husband. Especially as she now glanced worriedly at Seth's baby monitor, as if she could see him napping in his room through it.

Noah shook his head. He was being paranoid. Letting her fear outweigh his rational mind. He might have a bit of a soft spot for Addie and her boy, which he'd admit to no one ever, but he couldn't let her fears become his own.

She was his employee. If he sometimes caught himself watching her work in his kitchen… A housekeeper was all he needed. Less complicated than some of the other things his mind drifted to when he wasn't careful.

Luckily, Noah was exceedingly careful.

"Going to call in some backup to help me round them up."

"Shouldn't you call Laurel?" She paused when he scowled, but then continued. "Or anyone at the sheriff's department?"

She had a point, but he didn't want to draw attention to repeated issues at his ranch. Didn't want to draw the town's attention to Addie and that something might be going on, if it did in fact connect to her.

Maybe the smarter thing to do would be keep it all under wraps and then be more diligent, more watchful, and find whoever was pulling these little pranks himself. Mete out some Carson justice.

Yeah, he liked that idea a lot better.

"I'll handle it. Don't worry."

"Does this have to do with the poisoning? Do you think—"

Noah sent her a silencing look, trying not to feel guilty when she shrank back into the couch. "I'll handle it. Don't worry," he repeated.

She muttered something that sounded surprisingly sarcastic though he didn't catch the words, but she went back to folding the laundry and Noah crossed to the phone.

He called Ty first, then let Ty handle rounding up whatever Carsons could be of help. He didn't tell Ty about the footsteps, but a bit later when Ty, Grady and Clint showed up and Noah left the cabin with them, he held Grady back while Ty and Clint went to saddle their horses.

"What's up?" Grady asked. "You think this is connected to the poison?"

"I think I can't rule it out. I don't have a clue who's doing it, but part of me thinks it's some dumb kid trying to poke at a Carson to see what he'll do."

Grady laughed. "He'd have to be pretty dumb."

"Yeah. I don't want Addie to know, but…" He sighed. He needed someone besides him to know. Someone besides him on the watch, and Grady ran the one bar in town. He saw and heard things few other people in Bent did. "There were footprints at the window, as if someone had been watching her."

Grady's jaw tightened. "You think it's the ex?"

"I don't know what it is, but we need to keep an eye out."

Grady nodded. "I'll tell Laurel."

"No. She'll tell Addie. She's just calmed down from the poisoning—now this. I don't want to rile her more."

"Laurel will only do what's best. You know that."

Noah puffed out a breath. "Addie's settled from that skittish thing she was before. Hate to see her go back."

"She's not a horse, Noah." Grady grinned. "But maybe you know that all too well."

Noah scowled. "I want to know who poisoned my horses. I want to know who ran off my cattle, and I damn well want to know who's peeping in my window."

Grady nodded. "We'll get to the bottom of it. No one touches what's ours. Cow, mine or woman." Grady grinned at the old family joke.

Noah didn't. "No woman issues here," he grumbled. But Grady was right in one respect. No one messed with the Carsons of Bent, Wyoming, and walked away happy or satisfied about it. For over a century, the Carsons had been pitted on the wrong side of the law. The outlaws of Bent. The rich, law-abiding Delaneys had made sure that legend perpetuated, no matter what good came out of the Carson clan.

It was a good thing bad reputations could serve a purpose now and again. He'd do anything to protect what was his.

Addie wasn't his, though. No matter how he sometimes imagined she was.

He shook those thoughts away. "Will you stay here and watch out?"

"You could," Grady suggested.

"Addie'd think that's weird. I don't want her suspicious."

"That's an awful lot of concern for a Delaney, cousin," Grady said with one of his broad grins that were meant to irritate. Grady had perfected that kind of smile.

Noah knew arguing with Grady about the cause of his concern would only egg Grady on, so Noah grunted and headed for the stables.

Addie Foster was not his to protect personally. Grady'd do just as good a job, and Noah had cows to find and bring back home.

When that weird edge of guilt plagued him the rest of the night, as if his mission was to protect Addie and asking for help was some kind of failure, Noah had the uncomfortable feeling of not knowing what the hell to do about it.

When Noah didn't know how to fix a problem, he did the next best thing. He ignored it.

Chapter Three

November

Addie hummed along with the song playing over the speaker at the general store. Seth happily slammed his sippy cup against the sides of the cart as she unloaded the groceries onto the checkout counter.

"I swear he grows every week," Jen Delaney said with a smile as she began to ring up Addie's items.

"It's crazy. He's already in eighteen-month clothes." Addie bagged the groceries as Jen handed them to her.

It was true. Seth was growing like a weed, thriving in this life she'd built for them. Addie smiled to herself. After the horse poison and the fence debacle, things had settled down. She'd been here three months now. She had a routine down, knew many of the people in town and mostly had stopped looking over her shoulder at every stray noise. Sometimes nights were still hard, but for the most part, life was good. Really good.

Noah had assured her time and time again those two incidents were feud-related, nothing to do with her, and she was finally starting to believe him. She trusted Noah. Implicitly. With her safety, with Seth. Laurel had been right on that first car ride. Noah wasn't always easy to read or the warmest human being, but he was a *good* man.

Which had created something of a Noah situation. Well, more a weirdness than a situation. And a weirdness she was quite sure only she felt, because she doubted Noah felt much of anything for her. On the off chance he did, it was so buried she'd likely not live long enough to see it.

"Addie?"

Addie glanced up at Jen. The young woman must have finished ringing everything up while Addie was lost in Noah thoughts. Something that happened far too often as of late.

Addie paid for the groceries, smiling at Jen while she inwardly chastised herself.

Noah Carson was her boss. No matter that she liked the way he looked or that she got fluttery over his gentle way with the horses and cows. And Seth.

She sighed inwardly. He was so sweet with Seth. Never got frustrated with the boy's increasing mobility or fascination with Noah's hat or beard.

But no matter that Noah was sweet with Seth, or so kind with her, he was off-limits for her ever-growing fantasies of good, handsome men and happily-ever-afters.

She glanced down at the happy boy kicking in the cart. Sometimes Seth gave her that smile with big blue eyes and she missed her sister so much it hurt. But it always steadied her, renewed any resolve that needed renewing.

She would do anything to keep him safe.

She pushed the cart out of the general store to where her truck was parallel parked, but before she reached it, a man blocked her way.

She looked at him expectantly, waiting for him to move or say something, but he just stood there. Staring at her.

She didn't recognize him. Everything about him was nondescript and plain, and still he didn't move or speak.

"Excuse me," she finally said, pulling Seth

out of the cart and balancing him on her hip. "This is my truck."

The man moved only enough to glance at the truck. Also a new skill for her, driving a truck, but Noah had fixed up one of the old ones he used on the ranch for her to use when she had errands.

The strange man turned his gaze back to her and still said nothing. He still didn't move.

Addie's heart started beating too hard in her chest, fear seizing her limbs. This wasn't normal. This wasn't…

She turned quickly, her hand going over Seth's head with the idea of protecting him somehow. This man was here to get her. Peter had finally caught up with them. She had to run.

She could go back in the store and…and…

"Oof." Instead of her intended dash to the store, she slammed into a hard wall of man.

"Addie."

She looked up at Noah, whose hand curled around her arm. He looked down at her, something like concern or confusion hidden underneath all that hair and stoicism.

"Everything okay?" he asked in that gruff voice that suggested no actual interest in the answer, but that was the thing about Noah.

He gave the impression he didn't care about anything beyond his horses and cows, but he'd fixed up that truck for her even though she hadn't asked. He played with Seth as if people who hired housekeepers usually had relationships with the housekeeper's kid. He made sure there was food for Ty, room for Vanessa and Clint, and work if any of them wanted it.

He was a man who cared about a lot of people and hid it well.

"I just…" She looked back at where the strange, unspeaking man had been. There was no one there. No one. She didn't know how to explain it to Noah. She didn't know how to explain it to anyone.

The man hadn't said anything threatening. Hadn't done anything threatening, but that hadn't been normal. "I thought I saw someone…" She looked around again, but there was no sign of anyone in the sunshine-laden morning.

"As in *someone* someone?" Noah asked in that same stoic voice, and yet Addie had no doubt if she gave any hint of fear, Noah would jump into action.

So she forced herself to smile. "I'm being silly. It was just a man." She shook her head and gestured with her free hand. "I'm sure it was nothing." Which was a flat-out lie. As much as she'd love to tell herself it was nothing, she knew Peter too well to think this wasn't *something*.

She blew out a breath, scanning the road again. There was just no other explanation. He knew where she was. He knew.

"Addie."

She looked back at Noah, realizing his hand was still on her arm. Big and rough. Strong. Working for Noah had made her feel safe. Protected.

But this wasn't his fight, and she'd brought it to his door.

"I'm sorry," she whispered, closing her eyes.

"For what?" he asked in that gruff, irritable way.

Seth lunged for Noah, happily babbling his favorite word over and over again. "No, no, no." Addie tried to hold on to the wiggling child, but Noah took him out of her arms with ease.

"Aren't you supposed to be back at the ranch? You know I get groceries on Wednesdays. I could have picked up whatever for you."

"It's feed," Noah said. "Couldn't have loaded

it up yourself with the baby." He glanced at the grocery cart behind her. "We'll put the groceries in my truck."

"Oh, I can handle…"

"He always falls asleep on the way home, doesn't he?" Noah asked as if it wasn't *something* that he knew Seth's routine. Or that he was letting Seth pull the cowboy hat off his head, and then smash it back on.

Noah moved for the cart, because you didn't argue with Noah. He made a decision and you followed it whether you wanted to or not. Partly because he was her boss, but she also thought it was partly just him.

"Let's get home and you can tell me what really happened." Noah's dark gaze scanned the street as if he could figure everything out simply by looking around.

She knew it was foolish, but she was a little afraid he could. "I swear, nothing happened. I'm being silly."

"Well, you can tell me about that, too. At home." He handed her Seth and then took the cart.

Home. She'd wanted to build a *home*. For Seth. For herself. But if Peter had found her…

She couldn't let herself get worked up. For Seth's sake, she had to think clearly. She had to formulate a plan. And she couldn't possibly let Noah know the truth.

Noah didn't think running away was the answer, that she knew after listening to his lectures to Clint.

Beyond that, regardless of his personal feelings for her—whether they existed deep down or not—he had a very clear personal code. That personal code would never let a woman and a baby run away without protection.

Which would put him in danger. Very much because of her personal feelings, she couldn't let that happen.

"Okay. I'll meet you back at the ranch." She smiled pleasantly and even let him take the cart of groceries and wheel it down to where his truck was parked on the corner. She frowned at that. "If you were in town to pick up feed, why are you here?"

Noah didn't glance at her, but he did shrug. "Saw the truck. Thought you might need some help loading." Then he was hidden behind his truck door, loading the groceries into the back seat.

Addie glanced down at Seth. "I really don't know what to do with that man," she murmured, opening her own truck door and getting Seth situated in his car seat. She supposed in the end it didn't matter she didn't know what to do with him. If someone was here…

Well, Seth was her priority. She couldn't be a sitting duck, and she couldn't bring Noah into harm's way. This wasn't like the poison or the fence. This was directed at *her*. That man had stared at *her*. Whether or not those first two things were related didn't matter, because *this* was about *her*.

Which meant it was time to leave again. She slid into the driver's seat, glancing in her rearview mirror, where she watched Noah start walking back toward the store to return the now-empty cart.

Addie had become adept at lying in the past year. She'd *had* to, but mainly she only had to lie to strangers or people she didn't know very well. Even that initial lie to Laurel, and the past three months of upholding it with everyone, hadn't been hard. Pretending to be Seth's biological mother was as easy as pie since he was hers and hers alone these days.

But finding a new lie, and telling it to Noah's face—that was going to be a challenge. She changed her gaze from Noah's reflection to Seth in the car seat. She smiled at him in the mirror.

"It's okay, baby. I'll take care of it." Somehow. Someway.

NOAH HAD UNLOADED the groceries at the front door, and Addie had taken them inside, the baby monitor sitting on the kitchen table as they quietly worked.

He should have insisted they talk about what had transpired at the general store, but instead he'd gone back out to his truck and driven over to the barn to unload the feed.

Then he'd dawdled. He was not a man accustomed to dawdling. He was also not a man accustomed to *this*. Every time something bad had happened in the first two months, he'd been the one to find it. Little attacks that had been aimed at the ranch.

Whatever had shaken Addie today was about her. What she'd seen. He could attribute her shakiness to being "silly" as she said, or even her previous "situation" with her ex, but he didn't know what that was. Not really. He certainly hadn't poked into it. He was not a poker, and Addie was not a babbler. It was why this whole thing worked.

But she'd eased into life at the Carson

Ranch. So much so that Noah, on occasion, considered thanking Laurel and Grady for forcing his hand on the whole housekeeper thing. She'd made his life easier.

Except where she hadn't. Those uncomfortable truths he'd had to learn about himself— he was lonely, he liked having someone under his roof and to talk to for as little as he did it. He liked having her and Seth in particular.

Which was his own fault. She didn't carry any responsibility for his stupid feelings. Even if he'd had a sense of triumph over the fact Addie didn't jump at random noises anymore, and she didn't get scared for no reason. Both with the poison and the fence, she'd walked on eggshells for a few days, then gotten back to her old quietly cheerful self.

He'd never told her about the footprints and they'd never returned. So maybe he'd overreacted then. Maybe *he'd* been silly, but whatever had rattled her at the store was something real. Which meant they needed to talk about it.

But he wasn't the *talker.* He was the doer. Grady or Ty went in and did all the figuring out, and Noah brought up the rear, so to speak. He was there. He did what needed to be done, but he was no great determiner of what that thing was. He left that to people who liked to jack their jaw.

Which was when he realized what he really needed. He pulled his cell phone out of his pocket and typed a text. When he got the response he'd hoped for, he put his phone away and got back to his real work. Not protecting Addie Foster and whatever her issue was, but running a ranch.

He worked hard, thinking as little about Addie as possible, and didn't reappear at the main house until supper. He stepped up onto the porch, scraping the mud off his boots before entering.

The blast of warmth that hit him was an Addie thing. She opened the west-facing curtains so the sun set golden through the windows and into the kitchen and entryway every day. Whenever he stepped in, she had supper ready or almost.

Seth slammed his sippy cup against his high-chair tray and yelled, "No!" Noah was never sure if it was a greeting or an admonition.

Noah grunted at the boy, his favorite mode of greeting. He sneaked a glance at Addie to make sure she still had her back to him, then made a ridiculous face that made Seth squeal out a laugh.

Noah advanced closer, but he noted Addie was slamming things around in the kitchen and didn't turn to face him with her usual greeting and announcement of what was for dinner.

It all felt a little too domestic, which was becoming more and more of a problem. He couldn't complain about being fed nightly by a pretty woman, but sitting down with her and her kid for a meal every day was getting to feel normal.

Integral.

Noah hovered there, not quite sure what to do. Laurel had assured him via text she'd come in and figure out whatever was up with Addie after he'd contacted her, but Addie did not seem calmed.

He cleared his throat. "Uh. Um, need help?" he offered awkwardly.

She turned to face him, tongs in one hand and an anger he'd never seen simmering in her blue eyes.

She pointed the tongs at him. "You, Noah Carson, are a coward. And a bit of a high-handed jerk."

He raised an eyebrow at her, but Addie

didn't wilt. Not even a hint of backing down. She crossed her arms over her chest and stared right back at him. In another situation he might have been impressed at the way she'd blossomed into something fierce.

"Because?"

She huffed out a breath. "You went and told Laurel I was having a problem when I told you I was not."

"But you were."

"No. I wasn't." She pointed angrily at the table with the tongs. "Sit down and eat."

He'd never seen much of Addie's temper. Usually if she got irritated with him she went to some other room in the house and cleaned something. Or went into her room and played with Seth. She never actually directed any of her ire at him.

He didn't know what to do with it. But he *was* hungry, so he took his seat next to Seth's high chair, where the kid happily smacked his hands into the tiny pieces of food Addie had put on his tray before Noah walked in.

She slammed a plate in front of Noah. Chicken legs and mashed potatoes and some froufrou-looking salad thing. Usually she didn't *serve* him, but he wasn't one to argue with anyone, let alone an angry female.

She stomped back to the kitchen counter, then to the table again. She sat in a chair opposite him with an audible *thump*.

Her huffiness and sternness were starting to irritate him. He didn't have much of a temper beyond general curmudgeon, but when someone started poking at him, things tended to… Well, he tended to avoid people who made him lose his temper. Addie'd never even remotely tested that before.

But she sure was now.

"I can handle this," she said, leveling him with her sternest look. She shook out a paper towel and placed it on her lap like it was an expensive cloth napkin and they were in some upscale restaurant.

"What? What is this thing you can handle?" he returned evenly.

She stared right back at him like he was slow. "It's nothing. That's why I can handle it."

Noah wanted to beat his head against the table. "You were *visibly* shaken this morning, and it wasn't like it used to be."

Her sharp expression softened slightly. "What do you mean?"

Noah shrugged and turned his attention to his food. "When you first got here you were all jumpy-like. This was not the same thing."

She was quiet for a few seconds, so he took the opportunity to eat.

"I didn't know you noticed," she said softly.

He shrugged, shoveling mashed potatoes into his mouth and hoping this conversation was over.

He should have known better. Addie didn't poke at him, but she also didn't leave things unfinished. "I need you to promise you won't call Laurel like that again. The last thing I need is well-meaning people..." She trailed off for a few seconds until he looked up from his plate.

Her eyebrows were drawn together and she was frowning at her own plate, and Noah had the sinking, horrifying suspicion those were tears making her blue eyes look particularly shiny.

She cleared her throat. "I'll handle things. Don't bring Laurel into this again." She looked up, as if that was that.

"No."

"What did you say?" she asked incredulously.

"I said no."

She sputtered, something like a squeak emanating from her mouth. "You can't just...you can't just say no!"

"But I did."

Another squeaking sound, which Seth joined in as if it was a game.

Addie took a deep breath as if trying to calm herself. "A man stood in my way and wouldn't move. He said nothing, and he did nothing threatening. It was nothing. Calling Laurel, on the other hand, was something. And I did not appreciate it."

"If what happened this morning were nothing, it wouldn't have freaked you out. What did Laurel say?"

"She said you're an idiot and I should quit and move far away."

"No, she didn't." He didn't believe Laurel *would* say something like that, but there was a panicked feeling tightening his chest.

"Noah, this isn't your problem," Addie said, and if he wasn't crazy, there was a hint of desperation in her tone, which only served to assure him this *was* his problem.

"You live under my roof, Addie Foster. You are my problem."

She frowned at him as if that made no sense to her, but it didn't need to. It made sense to *him*. The people in his family and under his roof were under his protection. End of story.

Chapter Four

Addie ate the rest of her dinner in their normal quiet companionship. Quite honestly, she was rendered speechless by Noah's gruff, certain proclamation.

You are my problem.

He had no idea what kind of problem she could be if she stayed, and yet no matter how many times she'd chastised herself to pack up and leave *immediately*, here she was. Cleaning up dinner dishes while Seth crawled in and out of the play tent she'd placed on the floor for him.

You are my problem.

She glanced at the door. Noah had stridden back outside right after dinner, which he did sometimes. Chores to finish up or horses or cows to check on, though sometimes she thought he did it just to escape her.

She sighed heavily. Noah made no sense

to her, but she didn't want to be his *prob-lem*. He'd been nothing but kind, in fact proving to her that her sister's determination after Peter that all men were scum wasn't true in the least.

Noah might be hard to read and far too gruff, but he was the furthest thing from scum she'd ever met.

She glanced at Seth, who popped his smiling face out of the tent opening and screeched.

"Except for you, of course, baby," Addie said, grinning at Seth. Growing like a weed. It hurt to look at him sometimes, some mix of sorrow and joy causing an unbearable pain in her heart.

He'd settled in so well here. Their routine worked, and what would she do when she left? Where else would she find this kind of job where he got to be with her? Even if she could find a job that would allow her to afford day care, they wouldn't have the kind of security she needed. Seth always needed to be with her in case they needed to escape.

Like now.

She squeezed her eyes shut. She was in an impossible situation. She didn't want to put Noah—or any of the Carsons—at risk of

Peter, but if she ran away without thinking things through, she risked Seth's well-being.

"No! No! No!" Seth yelled happily, making a quick crawling beeline for the door.

Addie took a few steps before scooping Seth up into her arms, a wriggling mass of complaint.

"He's not back yet," Addie said gently, settling Seth on her hip as she moved to the windows to close the curtains for the night. Sometimes, though, she and Seth stood here and watched the stars wink and shimmer in the distance while they waited for Noah's last return of the evening.

It felt like home, this place. Even with a man whose life she didn't share and was her boss living under the same roof. It was all so *right*. How could she leave?

And how can you stay?

She shook her head against the thought and closed the curtains. As she stepped back toward the kitchen to gather Seth's tent, she noticed something on the floor.

An envelope. Odd. Dread skittered through her. Noah always brought the mail in when he came to grab lunch. He always put it in the same place. Which was most definitely not the floor.

Maybe it had fallen. Maybe someone had managed to shoehorn the envelope through the bottom of the door; most of the weather stripping was in desperate need of being replaced.

Her name was written in dark block letters. With no address. She swallowed, her body shaking against her will.

Seth wiggled in her arms and it was a good anchor to reality. She had a precious life to keep safe. Somehow. Someway. She was the only one who could.

She forced herself to bend down and place Seth gently on the floor. He crawled off for the tent, and with a shaking hand Addie picked up the envelope.

Slowly, she walked over to the table and sat down. She stared at it, willing her breathing to even and her hands to stop shaking. She'd open it, and then she'd know what her next move would have to be.

She forced one more breath in and out and then broke the seal of the envelope and pulled out the sheet of paper. Feeling sick to her stomach, Addie unfolded the paper until she could see text.

I see you, Addie.

She pressed her fingers to her mouth, willing herself not to break down. She'd come this far. She couldn't break down every time he found her. She just had to keep going, over and over again, until he didn't.

She wanted to drop the paper. Forget it existed. But she didn't have that option. She folded it back up and slid it inside the envelope, then pushed it into her pocket. She'd keep it. A reminder.

He wanted her scared. She didn't know why that seemed to be his priority when he could have her killed and take Seth far away.

There was no point trying to rationalize a sociopath's behavior. She knew one thing and one thing only: Peter wouldn't stop. So neither could she.

If she'd been alone, she might have risked staying in one spot. Just to see what he would do. But she wasn't alone. Now she had to protect Noah and the Carsons and Delaneys who'd been so kind to her.

She stood carefully, walking stiffly over to Seth. She pulled him out of the tent, much to his screaming dismay.

She patted his back. "Come on, baby. We don't have much time." She glanced at the windows where the curtains were now pulled.

Was he out there? Waiting for her? Was it all a lure to get her to come out?

Were his men out there? Oh, God, had they hurt Noah? True panic beat through her. She could escape. She'd had enough close calls— a landlord letting her know a man had broken into her apartment, noticing a broken motel window before she'd stepped inside—to know she could find her way out of this one.

But what if they'd hurt Noah? She couldn't leave him. She couldn't let them…

Seth was bucking and crying now, and Addie closed her eyes and tried to think. She couldn't rush out without thinking. She couldn't escape without making sure Noah was okay, which was not part of any of the escape plans she always had mapped out in the back of her mind.

She should call Laurel. She hated to call Laurel after yelling at Noah for doing so, but this wasn't about her pride or her secrets. It was about Noah's safety.

Seth was still screaming in her ear, kicking his little legs against her. Addie retraced her steps, perilously close to tears.

She made it to the kitchen and fumbled with the phone. She was halfway through dialing Laurel's number when the front door squeaked open. Addie dropped the phone, scanning the kitchen for a weapon, any weapon.

If she could make it two feet, there was a butcher knife. Not much of a weapon against a gun, but—

Noah stepped inside, alone, his dark cowboy hat covering most of his face as he stomped his boots on the mat. When he glanced up at her, her relief was short lived, because there was a trickle of blood down his temple and cheek.

Addie rushed over to him, Seth's tantrum finally over. "Oh, my God, Noah." He was okay. Bleeding, but okay. She flung herself at him, relief so palpable it nearly toppled her. "You're okay," she said, hugging Seth between them.

"What the hell is wrong with you?" Noah grumbled, a hard wall against her cheek.

Which was when she realized she'd miscalculated deeply. Because he would know everything was wrong now, and she had no way of brushing this off as being silly.

HE FELT ADDIE stiffen against him and then slowly pull away. She did not meet his gaze, and she did not answer his question.

He was a little too disappointed she wasn't holding on to him anymore. "Addie," he warned, too sharp and gruff. But the woman affected him and he didn't know how to be soft about it. "What is it?"

"You're…bleeding," she offered weakly, still not looking at him.

"Yeah, one of my idiot cousins left a shovel in the middle of the yard and I tripped right into the barn door. What's going on? And don't lie to me. Just be honest. I'm not in the mood to play detective."

"Are you ever in the mood for anything?" she muttered while walking away from him, clearly not expecting him to catch her words.

"You'd be surprised," he returned, somewhat gratified when she winced and blushed. Still expressly not looking at him. It grated. That she was lying to him. That today was one big old ball of screwy.

That when she'd thrown herself at him he'd wanted to wrap his arms around her and hold her there. Worst of all, her *and* the kid.

"So, I just thought… I thought I heard something and—"

"Bull." Did she have any idea what a terrible liar she was? It was all darting eyes and nervous hand-wringing.

"Well, I mean, maybe I didn't hear anything, but when I was closing the windows there was a bird and—"

"Bull."

She stomped her foot impatiently. "Stop it, Noah."

"Stop feeding me bull and I'll stop interrupting."

She frowned at him and shook her head and heaved an unsteady exhale. She looked frazzled and haunted, really. Haunted like she'd been when she'd first gotten here, but he'd never seen her look panicked.

She walked over to the tiny kitchen, where Seth's tent was on the floor. She crouched down and let the boy crawl inside. She watched the kid for a second before walking over to a drawer and pulling out a washcloth. She wet it at the sink, then moved to the cabinet above the oven where they kept a few first aid things and medicine. She grabbed a bandage before returning to him.

She stood in front of him, gaze unreadable on his. She stepped close—too close, because he could smell dinner and Seth's wipes on her. That shouldn't be somehow enticing. He wasn't desperate for some domestic side of his life.

But she got up on her tiptoes and placed the warm cloth to where he'd scraped his forehead on the edge of the door. She wiped at the cut, her gaze not leaving his until she had to open the bandage.

Her eyebrows drew together as she peeled it from its plastic and then smoothed it over his forehead, her fingertips cool and soft against his brow. She met his gaze again then, sadness infusing her features.

"Noah, I have to leave."

He studied her, so imploringly serious, and, yeah, he didn't think that was bull. "Why?"

She glanced back at Seth, who was slapping his hands happily against the floor. "I just do. I can't give any kind of notice or time to find a new housekeeper. I have to go now." She glanced at the window, vulnerability written into every inch of her face that usually would have made Noah take a big old step back. He didn't do fragile, not a big, rough man like him.

But this wasn't about smoothing things over. This was about protecting someone who was very clearly in trouble.

"You're not going anywhere. You just need to tell me what's going on and we'll figure it out."

She looked back at him, expression bleak and confused. "Why?"

"Why?" He wanted to swear, but he thought better of it as Seth crawled over to his feet and used Noah's leg to pull himself into a standing position. Addie needed some reassuring, some soft and kind words, and he was so not the man for that.

But he was the only man here, and from everything Laurel and Grady had told him, and from Addie's own actions, Noah could only assume she'd been knocked around by Seth's father and feared him even now.

Softness might not be in him, but neither was turning away from something a little wounded.

"You're a part of the house. You've made yourself indispensable," he continued, trying to wipe that confused bleakness off her face.

"No. No. No," Seth babbled, hitting Noah's leg with his pudgy baby fingers.

Noah scooped the kid up into his arms, irritated that Addie was still standing there staring at him all big-eyed and beautiful and hell if he knew what to do with any of this.

"You didn't just take a job when you came here—you joined a family," he said harshly. "We protect our own. That wasn't bull I was feeding you earlier. That is how things work here. You're under Carson protection."

"I've never known anyone like you," she whispered. Before that bloomed too big and warm and stupid in his chest, she kept going. "Any of you. Laurel, Grady. Jen, Ty. The whole lot of you, and it's so funny the town is always going on about some feud and Grady and Laurel cursing everything, but you're all the same, all of you Carsons and Delaneys. So good and wanting to help people who shouldn't mean anything to you."

"You've been here too long for that to be true. Of course you mean something to us." He cleared his throat. "Besides, you're a Delaney yourself by blood."

She looked away for a second, and he couldn't read her expression but Seth made a lunge for her. One of his favorite games to play, lunging back and forth between them. Over and over again.

Addie took Seth, but she met Noah's gaze with a soft, resigned sadness. "I'm not safe here. More importantly, Seth isn't safe here. We have to go."

"Where?"

"What?"

"Where will you go that you'll be safe?"

"I…" She blew out a breath, that sheen of tears filling her eyes, and if this hadn't been so serious, he would have up and walked away. He didn't do tears.

But this was too big. Too important.

"I don't know," she whispered, one of the tears falling over her cheek. "I'm not sure anywhere will ever be safe."

Noah had the oddest urge to reach out and brush it away. He tamped that urge down and focused on what needed to be done. "Then you'll stay."

"Noah."

"If you don't know where to be safe, then you'll stay here where a whole group of people are ready and willing to protect you and Seth."

"I can't put any of you in this, Noah. It's dangerous."

"Not if you tell us what we're up against." Not that it'd change *his* mind. He'd fight a whole damn army to keep her here.

Because she was useful. Like he'd said before. Integral. To his house. To the ranch. That was all.

"Promise me you'll stay put." They were too close, standing here like this. Even as Seth bounced in her arms and reached for his hat, their eyes didn't leave each other.

But she shook her head. "I can't, Noah. I can't promise you that."

Chapter Five

Addie knew the next step was to walk away. Run away, but Noah's gaze held her stuck. She was afraid to break it, that doing so might break her.

She'd been strong for so long, alone for so long. She had to keep being that, but the allure of someone helping... It physically hurt to know she couldn't allow herself that luxury.

"Here are your choices," Noah said in that low, steady voice that somehow eased the jangling nerves in her gut. "You can try to run away, and I can call every Carson, hell, *and* Delaney, in a fifty-mile radius and you won't get two feet past the town limits."

Irritation spiked through her. "Noah, you—"

"Or you can sit down and tell me what's going on and we can fight it. Together."

Together.

She couldn't wrap her mind around this. Protection and together. Because she was his employee? Because she lived under his roof? It didn't make any kind of sense.

Her father had cut off Kelly when she'd dropped out of school and refused to work at the furniture store. Then when she'd asked him for help in Kelly's final trimester when the depth of her trouble with Peter was really sinking in, he'd refused to help.

He'd told Addie to never come home again if she was going to help Kelly.

If a father had so little love for his daughters, why was a friend, at best, so willing to risk himself to protect her?

"Telling me would be much easier," Noah said drily.

It sparked a lick of irritation through her. She didn't care for this man of such few words ordering her around. "You don't get to tell me what to do. You aren't my keeper. You aren't even…" She trailed off, because it wasn't true. No matter how quiet and stoic he could be, he *had* become her friend. Someone she relied on. Someone she worked *with* to keep the Carson Ranch running. It had given her so much in three short months, and she'd pictured Seth growing up here, right here. A good man.

Just like Noah.

Noah *was* her friend. Something like a partner, and wouldn't that be nice? Wouldn't that make all this seem possible? Which was why she couldn't. She just couldn't. She'd made a promise to herself. No one else got hurt in this.

"Noah, the truth is, I care about you." Far more than she should. "I care about all of you—Laurel and Grady and Jen and…the lot of you who've made me feel like this was home." She glanced toward the window, but she'd closed the curtains. Was someone out there? Waiting? Would they attack? "But the kind of danger I'm in is the kind I can't bring on all your heads. I couldn't live with myself."

"I don't think that's true," he said, still standing so close and so immovable. Like he could take on the evil that was after her. "I think you'd do anything, risk anything, to keep Seth safe."

Her chest felt like it was caving in. Because he was right. She would do anything. She didn't want to bring the people who'd been so good to her into the middle of it, but what if it was the best bet to keep Seth safe?

"And so would I," he continued. "No little kid deserves to live in the shadow of the threat of violence, so we don't run. *You* don't run. We fight it. But I need to know what I'm fighting."

What was there to do in the face of Noah's mountain wall of certainty and strength? She didn't have any power against it. Not when she could all but feel the determination coming off him in waves. Not when he let Seth gleefully fall into his arms, and there was so much danger outside these walls.

"Seth's father is a dangerous man," she whispered. She knew *that* was obvious and yet saying it out loud…

"He knocked you around."

He said it like a statement, and maybe she should treat it like a question and refute it. But what was the point? "He's a mobster." She laughed bitterly. "I didn't believe it the first time someone told me. As if mobsters are real."

"But he is."

Noah's voice was serious. Not a hint of mocking or disbelief. Which hurt, because when Kelly had told her about Peter's criminal ties, over a year ago, Addie had laughed it off. Then, she'd figured they'd call the cops.

It had taken Kelly's death for Addie to finally get it through her head.

Kelly had been talking about going to the cops, telling them what little she knew. The very day after she'd told Addie that, she'd been shot and killed on her way home from the drugstore.

A mugging gone wrong, the police had told Addie.

But Kelly had been certain she was in danger and in that moment Addie had finally gotten it through her thick skull that Peter was not the kind of man who was ever going to pay for his crimes or listen to reason.

He was a murderer and she couldn't stop him.

Kelly had kept Seth a secret, or so Addie had thought. But she'd gotten Peter's first note ten minutes after the police had left her apartment informing her of Kelly's murder.

Too bad.

She hadn't understood at first. Then she'd gotten the next a month later.

We're watching.

She'd taken it to the police, but they'd decided it was a prank.

The next month's letter arrived and had prompted Addie's flight reflex.

We're coming for my son. And you.

Peter was dangerous, and there was nothing…*nothing* she could do to stop him. Laws didn't matter—the police had never helped her, and once he'd involved Seth she couldn't trust law enforcement not to take Seth away from her.

Right or good certainly didn't matter when it came to Peter *or* the law.

"He could have me killed and Seth taken away with the snap of a finger. But he doesn't. I don't know what game he's playing. I only know I have to keep Seth safe. I thought we'd be safe here. Too isolated for even him to find, but I was an idiot. And now we have to leave."

"You won't be leaving."

She looked up at him, wondering what combination of words it would take, because he didn't understand. Maybe he wasn't scoffing at the idea of the mob, but he didn't truly get it if he thought he could keep her protected. "Noah, the cops couldn't help…" She almost mentioned Kelly, but she couldn't tell him about Kelly. Couldn't tell him she couldn't go to the police regarding Seth because she technically had no rights over her sister's child. "…me. I tried. Who are you to stop him? I realize you and the Carsons fancy yourselves tough, Wild West outlaws, but you cannot fight the *mob*."

"I don't see why not."

She blinked at him. "You have a screw loose."

His mouth quirked, that tiny hint of a smile she so rarely got out of him, and usually only aided by Seth. All hopes of more of Noah's smiles were gone. Dead. She had to accept it. She couldn't let him change her mind.

"I don't want you hurt," she whispered, all the fear welling up inside her. "I don't want anyone getting hurt."

"Same goes, Addie." He had started to lean back and forth on his heels as Seth dozed on his shoulder.

It was such a sight, this big, bearded, painfully tough man cradling a small child to his chest. They were both in so much danger and she didn't know how to fix any of it.

"It's late. Let's get some sleep tonight. I'll call up Grady and Ty in the morning and we'll plan."

"Plan what?"

"How to keep you and Seth safe." He rubbed his big, scarred hand up and down Seth's back.

"They're here, Noah." Her voice broke, and

she'd worry about embarrassment later. "They left me a note. They're *here*. We don't have time for plans."

She hadn't realized a tear escaped her tightly and barely held control until Noah reached out, his rough hand a featherlight brush against her cheek, wiping the tear away.

"Then we'll have to fight."

TRUTH BE TOLD, Noah didn't know what a man was supposed to do when a woman told him the mob was after her, but he'd learned a long time ago that in the face of a threat, you always pretended you knew what you were doing.

"Show me the note."

She backed away then, though not far. He didn't think even at her most scared she'd back away from the baby sleeping in his arms. Seth was a nice weight. Warm and important.

"Show me the note," he repeated, in the same quiet but certain tone. The kind of tone he'd employ with a skittish horse and not, say, how he'd speak to his teenage cousin who annoyed the piss out of him.

She inhaled sharply, but he watched the way she let it out. Carefully. Purposefully. She was scared witless, but she was handling it. Though he'd grown to know her, respect her even, the way she was handling this without falling apart was surprising him.

She reached behind her and pulled out an envelope. "It was…" She paused and cleared her throat. She'd cried a few moments ago, just a few tears, and it cracked something inside him. But she was handling it now. Holding her own. Against the threat of a *mobster*.

"It was on the floor. I assume slipped under the door." Her face paled. "God, I hope that's how it got in here."

Noah kept his expression stoic and his gaze on her, though now he wanted to search the house from top to bottom. Too many nooks and crannies. Too many…

One thing at a time. That's how things got built and solved. One thing at a time.

Her hand was shaking as she held out the envelope. He could see her name written there. Addie Foster. Yet it didn't matter what was in the letter. It mattered that Addie get it through her head he was going to protect her.

He put his hand over her shaking one. "Let's go to your room. We'll put Seth down, and then I'll make sure the house is secure." He'd call Laurel, and she could decide how involved the police needed to be. "You know

Laurel's a cop, right? A good one." He nudged her toward the hall.

"I'm sure she is," Addie replied, gaze darting everywhere as they walked back toward the bedrooms. "But the law can't touch him."

"That might be true back where you're from, but it ain't true here."

She looked at him bleakly as they stepped into her room. "It's true everywhere."

Noah was not a demonstrative person by any stretch of the imagination, but he had the oddest urge to pull her to his chest. Let her nestle right there where the baby was sleeping.

Instead, he turned to the crib and transferred Seth onto the mattress. The baby screwed up his mouth, then brought his thumb into it and relaxed. Within moments his eyes drooped shut and his breathing evened.

Noah glanced around the room. Nothing was amiss, and he knew for a fact the window didn't open. It'd accidentally been painted shut two years ago, and they'd left it that way so they had a room to put Clint in he couldn't escape without going through one of the main thoroughfares.

The joy of teenagers.

So, one room checked out and safe. Addie

stood next to her bed, arms wrapped around herself, envelope clutched in one hand. She shook from head to toe. And why wouldn't she? She'd been running from a mobster for how long?

Noah'd be damned if she ran another mile.

He eased the note from her grasp and then pulled the letter from the envelope.

I see you, Addie.

He muttered something particularly foul since the baby was too fast asleep to hear him. "I'm going to call Laurel." She opened her mouth to argue, no doubt, but he kept going. "I'm going to check out the house. I want you to stay put, door locked, until I'm sure everything is secure." She wanted to argue, he could see it all over her, so he played dirty. "You're in charge of Seth. Stay put."

"I know you want to help," she said, her voice raspy with emotion. "I also know you think you *can* help." She shook her head. "You don't know what you're up against."

It poked at the Carson pride he didn't like to put too much stock in, but Carsons had survived centuries of being the poor-as-dirt underdog in the fight. Carsons always found a way to make it work, and even a mobster wouldn't make that different. "And you don't know what or *who* you've got in your corner."

She visibly swallowed. "I'm afraid, Noah, and I don't know how not to be. He killed my sister. Seth's father had her *killed*. I've taken his son from him. I'll be lucky if all he does is kill me, too."

He couldn't stomach the thought, and it was that horrible, clutching panic that moved him, that had him acting with uncharacteristic emotion. He touched her, too-rough hands curling around her shoulders. His grip was too tight. She was too fragile, and yet she didn't wince or back away.

Because she wasn't actually fragile. He thought of that first moment he'd seen her, when he'd been so sure. He'd been wrong. She was brave and bone-deep strong.

She looked up at him, all fear and hope.

"He will not lay a hand on you," Noah growled. "Not a finger. This is Bent, Wyoming, and we make some of our own rules out here. Especially when Carsons and Delaneys are involved. Now, you sit. Maybe make a list of all the players so Laurel knows who she's looking for, and try to remember in detail everything that's happened with Seth's father so far. I'm going to search the house and once I know we're safe in here, we'll come up with a plan to stop him where he stands."

"If we escalate, he escalates," Addie said miserably.

"Then we'll escalate until it's finished. You're done running, Addie Foster. You belong right here." He'd do whatever it took to make that true.

Chapter Six

Addie's eyes were gritty from lack of sleep and her throat ached from talking. Far as she could tell, she'd told her story—well, a version of it—four times. Noah first, then once to Laurel and Grady, once to Noah's brother, Ty—who apparently had been an Army Ranger. Then she'd spouted the story all over again to a youngish-looking deputy in uniform.

She left out the fact Seth wasn't hers. If Peter being in the mob didn't matter here, maybe Seth's parentage didn't, either.

After the whole endless rehashing of it, Laurel and the other deputy, followed by Noah, Grady and Ty, had gone out to search the property. Noah's cousin Vanessa had arrived to watch after Addie.

"You're babysitting me," Addie said, watching the woman move around the kitchen.

"Babysitting happens when you've got a mobster after you, I think."

Fair enough.

Addie imagined Vanessa Carson was the kind of woman who'd know how to handle this on her own. She looked as infinitely tough as her brother, Grady, and male cousins. She had the same sharpness to her features, and there was the way she held herself. Like she knew she was right and she'd fight to the death to prove it.

Addie wanted so badly to believe the Carsons could take on Peter and his thugs.

But *why*? No matter how often Noah told her he'd protect her, she couldn't figure out *why*.

"This is an awful lot of manpower for the maid," Addie said, a comment she might have swallowed if she hadn't been exhausted, nerves strung taut. She stared miserably at Seth's monitor. He'd wake up soon, and how was she going to take care of him without falling apart?

The same way you've been doing for the past year. You're strong, too, whether you feel that way or not.

She liked to think of that as her sister's voice urging her on, but she knew it was just herself. Kelly had always had more of a glass-is-half-empty outlook on life.

"But you aren't just a maid," Vanessa said, as if it wasn't even a question. "Noah runs the ranch, you run the house. That's a partnership, at least—Noah'd see it that way. Noah doesn't just *employ* people. He collects them."

When Addie only stared at Vanessa, trying to work that out, Vanessa sighed and walked over to the table, taking the seat across from Addie.

"Noah's got a soft heart. I think that's why he hides it all with beard and grunts. I think some people were just born that way. Protectors. He doesn't see it as a debt to be paid, or an inconvenience. Once you're in his orbit, you're his. Even if he doesn't like you much."

"That doesn't make any sense."

Vanessa laughed, low and rumbly, just like the rest of the Carsons. "I've never thought Noah made much sense, so I agree. But it doesn't have to. It's who he is. It's what he does. You know, Noah's a firm believer in this feud business between the Carsons and the Delaneys. Delaneys are always out to get us, and messing with that is a historical recipe for disaster."

"But—"

Vanessa held up a hand. "When Laurel was in some trouble before you moved here, Noah jumped right in to help. When Grady announced he and Laurel were shacking up…" Vanessa shuddered. "He was the only one who didn't make a loud, raucous argument against it."

"I think they're sweet," Addie whispered, staring at the table. Even though it wasn't the point. Even though her heart beat painfully in her chest. Noah was unlike any man she'd ever known.

How differently things would have turned out for her and her sister if they'd had more honorable men in their lives.

"Of course you do," Vanessa returned. "You're a Delaney."

Addie looked up at Vanessa's sharp face, because she didn't particularly consider herself family. "I guess, along the line, but—"

"Here? Along the line counts."

"So Noah thinks I'm cursed, but he'll protect me anyway?"

"He will."

"But he'll never see beyond the fact I'm a Delaney?" Another thing she shouldn't have said. What did it matter what he saw her as?

She was just his maid, even if that meant she'd fallen into the path of his protection.

"Now, that is an interesting question," Vanessa drawled. "If we weren't worried about mobsters and such, I'd probably—"

A faint sound staticked through the monitor. Both Vanessa and Addie looked at it. Then another sound.

"It sounds like someone's—"

"Breathing," Vanessa finished for her, and then they were both on their feet, scrambling toward the room.

It could have been Seth, having a bad dream, puffing out those audible gasps of air. But she knew what her baby sounded like. Knew what odd noises the monitor picked up. This was not that.

Vanessa reached the door first, pulling a small gun out of the inside pocket of her jacket. "If someone's there, you let me deal. You get the baby and get out."

Addie nodded as an icy, bitter calm settled over her. She didn't have time to be afraid. She could only focus on saving Seth.

Vanessa quietly and carefully turned the knob, then flung open the door in a quick, loud movement.

There was a figure in the window. Addie

didn't have time to scream or panic. She rushed to Seth's crib and pulled him into her arms. She couldn't hear anything except the beating of her heart as she held Seth close, too close. He wiggled and whimpered sleepily.

It was only with him safely held to her chest that Addie realized there was shouting coming from outside. Vanessa was standing on the rocking chair, peering out what appeared to be a hole cut in the glass of the window.

"What happened?" Addie asked, her voice no more than a croak. Safe. Safe. Seth was safe. It was paramount.

Vanessa glanced back at her. "They got him. Laurel's arresting him."

"Who—"

Noah barreled in through the door, all gasping breath and wild eyes. Addie had never seen him in such a state, and she didn't even get a word out before he grabbed her. *Grabbed* her, by the arms, searching her face as Seth wriggled between them. It was the most emotion she'd ever seen on the man.

"You're both all right?"

Addie nodded wordlessly. She didn't know what to say to him when he was touching her like this, looking at her like this. It was more than just that stoic certainty that he'd protect her. So much more.

"I'm good, too," Vanessa quipped.

"Shut up," Noah snapped, seeming to remember himself. He dropped Addie's shoulders as though they were hot coals. He stepped back, raking a hand through his hair, his face returning to its normal impassive state.

It was as if that simple motion locked all that *feeling* that had been clear as day on his face back down where it normally went.

If there weren't a million other things to worry about, she might have been thrilled to see that much emotion geared toward her.

"Who was it? What happened?" Addie asked, cradling Seth's small head with her hand.

"As to who, we're not sure. He's not talking. No ID. We'd canvassed the buildings. Ranch is too big in the dark to find anyone. We were coming back when I caught the figure at your window. We all ran over, pulled him out, Laurel cuffed him. She'll take him down to the station now. She wanted you to come out and see if you could ID him first."

It was all so much, and she knew they wouldn't understand it was only the beginning. This was only the first wave. Peter would keep coming, wave after wave, until she had no strength or sanity left. That's when he'd take Seth. When she was at her weakest.

She swallowed against the fear, the futility. She wouldn't let it happen.

She was a Delaney, apparently, and she had a Carson—or four—in her corner. Noah—all that worry and fear and determination and vengeance flashing in his eyes for that brief minute—was in her corner.

They would keep Seth safe. *They* could.

HE DIDN'T WALK Addie outside to ID the guy. Couldn't manage it. Not with all the awful things roiling in his gut. If he went out there, he wasn't certain he'd control himself around the man who'd been breaking into his house.

So he sent her with Vanessa. He held Seth, the boy back asleep again despite the commotion. Noah studied the room he'd thought was safe, glared at the window where a carefully cut circle gave adequate access for a small man to try to crawl through.

She couldn't sleep here tonight. It wasn't safe. No room with windows was safe, it seemed, and *all* the rooms had windows. Nothing was safe.

He ran his free hand over his face. What a mess.

But it wasn't an insurmountable mess. They'd caught this guy, and Noah was under no illusions it was the mobster after Addie and Seth, but he worked for him. He had to have information, and with information, they could keep Addie safe.

She had two families ready to take up arms and keep her and the kid safe. He had to let that settle him.

Addie returned, clearly beaten down. "It wasn't the same man from the store. So Peter has two men here. Usually he only sends one." She looked exhausted and all too resigned to a negative fate.

Not on his watch.

"You can't stay here," he said when she didn't offer anything.

Her entire face blanched in a second. "But you said..." She looked around the room desperately, then straightened her shoulders and firmed her mouth. "Well, fine, then, better to have a running start."

"Running?" He stepped toward her, lowering his voice when Seth whimpered into his shoulder. "Where the hell do you think you're going?"

She fisted her hands on her hips, that flash of temper from before at dinner. He was glad to see it now. Better than resigned.

"You just told me I can't stay here!"

"*Here*. In this room."

She blinked. "Oh." She cleared her throat. "Be more specific next time."

That she could even think he was kicking her out…

Everything in him ached, demanded he touch her, but he kept the impulse in check. "Nothing that happens is going to change the fact that we're in this together."

"Noah…" She bit her lip and took a few steps closer to him. She seemed to be studying him. His eyes. His mouth.

My damn soul.

"You were so worried," she said, her voice hushed and nearly awed. "When you came in here. About me. About Seth."

"Of course I was. A man was climbing in your window. You were being threatened in *my* house. What man wouldn't be worried?"

"Because it's your house?"

She was fishing, he realized with a start. Fishing for more. It was his turn to swallow, and he was man enough to admit he backed away. Sometimes a man had to tactically retreat.

She didn't let him. She took those steps he'd backed off, closing the necessary distance between them. He thought for a blinding second she was going to reach out to touch him.

Instead, her fingertips brushed Seth's cheek. "I wish I understood you." She looked up, dark blue eyes too darn perceptive for any man's good. "I wish I understood what makes a man think people are his possessions to control, to warp, to let live and die at will, and what makes a man protect what isn't even his."

You are *mine*.

It was a stupid thought to have and he needed to get rid of it.

"We need to figure out what we're going to do. We need to formulate a plan. This house isn't safe, but I don't know where else would be safe."

Addie turned away from him then. He wished he could erase her fear. But he knew even when you were afraid and had someone protecting you, someone helping you, it couldn't eradicate fear. Fear was a poison.

But it could also be the foundation. He'd lived in fear and learned to protect out of it. So he would figure out a way to protect her.

"There's a cabin," he continued. "It's well-known Carson property and it's entirely possible that since someone tracked you here, they could track you there. But it's smaller. We could protect it better."

"We?" She turned around again. "Noah, what about the ranch?"

"Grady and Ty can take care of the ranch. And Vanessa, if necessary. I have plenty of help to carry out the day-to-day, and to keep an eye out in case any other uninvited guests show up."

She shook her head vigorously. "You can't leave your ranch. It's your work. It's your home."

It was. His heart and soul. But he could hardly send her off alone, and he'd be damned if he sent her with anyone else.

"We'll go. Until we get some information from Laurel about who this guy is and what he's doing. We'll go. You'll be safe there. Seth will be safe there, and we'll figure something out. A plan."

"Now?"

Noah nodded firmly. "Pack up whatever you need for yourself and for Seth. I'll make arrangements."

"Noah."

He told himself one of these days he would get that wary bafflement off her face. But for now, there was too much work to do.

"I don't know how to thank you. I don't know how to..." Her gaze moved from his face to the little boy in his arms. "You've been so good to us."

"It sounds like you deserve a little of people being good to you."

She nodded. "Deserve." She blew out a breath and he could see the exhaustion and stress piling on top of her, but she was still standing. He remembered that first moment, when he'd been irritated Grady and Laurel had thrust someone fragile on him.

But Addie had turned out to be something else entirely, and he would do whatever it took to ease some of that exhaustion from her. Get her out of here now, and then once they got to the cabin she could sleep. Rest. He'd take care of everything.

"I will keep you safe. I promise you." She didn't believe him yet. He didn't need her to, but he'd keep saying it until she did.

She stared up at him and reached out. He thought she was going to take Seth, or gently brush the baby's cheek again, but this time she touched *him*. Her fingertips brushed his bearded jaw. "I know you want to."

"I will. I don't make promises I can't keep."

Her mouth curved the slightest bit, but Noah couldn't catch a breath because she was still touching him. She traced the line of his jaw to his chin, then back up the other side, and no amount of stoicism he'd adopted over the years could keep the slight hitch out of his breathing.

Her smile grew. "I believe that," she said, watching her own hand as it traveled down to rest on his chest, just above his heart.

She looked up at him from underneath her lashes, and it wasn't the first time in three months he'd wanted to kiss her, but it was the first time in three months it seemed right. Possible. Infinitely necessary.

He shifted Seth easily, carefully, and if he leaned toward Addie's pretty, lush mouth, well, he was a man, damn it. Who could deny this attraction when they were both exhausted and scared to their boots?

The door swung open and Addie jumped

back. Noah had some presence of mind. He simply glared at their intruder.

"Hey, you guys ever com…" Ty trailed off, looking from Noah to Addie, and then back again with a considering glance. "Sorry to interrupt."

"Weren't," Noah returned, that one word all he could manage out of his constricted throat at first. "I'm going to take Addie to the cabin."

Ty nodded. "Good idea. Safer. Less room to watch. Grady, Vanessa and I will handle things here."

Noah jerked his head in assent. "Let's move fast."

Chapter Seven

Addie slept like the dead. No matter how many fears or worries occupied her brain, she'd been up for nearly twenty-four hours by the time they reached the isolated Carson cabin.

And, she supposed, as she awoke slowly in an unfamiliar bed in an unfamiliar house, knowing Noah was nearby keeping her safe had made sleep easy.

She stretched in the surprisingly comfy bed. Surprising because everything about the Carson cabin was rustic and sparse, but the bed was nice.

She had to get out of it, though, because Noah would need some sleep. He'd probably been up before her yesterday, and now he'd spent who knew how long taking care of Seth and keeping them safe.

She pressed her hand against her chest. It

simply ached at how much that meant. How much she'd wanted to kiss him last night. Or this morning. Whatever moment in time. He'd been about to. She'd almost been sure of it.

Almost.

She pushed out of the bed. She hadn't even changed out of her jeans and T-shirt last night. She'd fallen into that bed, making noises about when Seth would wake up and need a diaper change, and Noah had hushed her, and that was the last thing she remembered.

She ran a hand through her hair. It'd be good to tidy up, but she had no idea how long she'd slept. There was no clock in here, the window was boarded up and she had no idea where she'd left her phone.

She opened the bedroom door and stepped into basically the rest of the cabin. A small living room, an even smaller kitchen that attached, and a bathroom on the other side. There was another door she had to assume was another bedroom.

The diminutive size of the place made it far more secure than the ranch. Just as isolated, of course, but there wasn't much in Bent by way of bustling cosmopolitans.

She frowned at the empty room. The front door was locked shut. Multiple times. A door lock, a dead bolt, a padlock on some latch-looking thing. It was dark because all the windows were boarded up. Surely Noah couldn't have done all that while she was sleeping.

And where *was* he?

It was then she heard the faint snore. She pivoted so she could see the front of the couch, and there was all six-foot-who-knew of Noah Carson, stretched out on a tiny couch, a cowboy hat over his face, while Seth slept just as soundlessly in the little mobile crib, Noah's arm draped over the side—his fingertips touching Seth's leg.

It was too much, the way this big, gruff cowboy had taken to a small child who wasn't even his. But Addie understood that. Seth was her nephew, not her own, but he was hers now. All hers.

Noah wanted to protect her and Seth, but he was putting himself in danger to do so. He was even changing his life, for however brief a time, to do so.

So she would protect him right back. Take care of him as much as he'd allow.

She tiptoed to the kitchen and started poking around the cabinets seeing what kind of provisions they had. She knew Noah had packed a lot of things before they'd loaded up Vanessa's small car—an attempt at throwing anyone who might be watching off the scent—and drove up the mountains in the starry dark to this place. Vanessa had driven off so no evidence would be left that the cabin was occupied, and then it'd just been her and Noah and Seth.

She blew out a breath. *Breakfast.* She needed to focus on the here and now, not what came before and not what would come after. She looked around for her phone, found it on the small kitchen counter.

She flipped it open, searching for the time, only to see the text message from a Boston-area number.

Her stomach turned. She'd gotten a new burner phone in every city she'd stayed in for a while, but Peter somehow always found out what her number was.

She wanted to delete the message before looking at it, because she knew it would say something awful. Something that would haunt her. She remembered each and every one of his previous messages, and how many had made her run again.

All the words of the terrible things he was going to do to her once he found her that she'd read months and months ago swirled around in her head. She couldn't erase them.

But she could erase this message.

"What's wrong?"

Addie jumped a foot, not having realized Noah had woken up and was peering at her over the back of the couch.

"Nothing," she said automatically.

"Addie, I know you're scared, but you have to be honest with me if we are going to do this. There can't be any lies between us anymore."

She glanced at the crib where Seth was still sleeping. Was the fact that Seth wasn't her child a lie? How could it be? He was hers now. One way or another.

Then she glanced at the phone in her hand.

"It might be nothing," she said hopefully. She didn't believe it was nothing. There wasn't anything *nothing* about a Boston area code texting a number she'd given no one except Carsons and Delaneys.

Noah stood. He skirted the couch and raked fingers through his hair. It was sleep tousled and all too appealing. Even with the awful fear and panic fluttering in her breast, she looked at him and there was this soothing to all those awful jitters. They still existed, fear and worry, but it was like they were wrapped up in the warm blanket of Noah's certainty.

Noah's certainty, which existed around him like his handsomeness. Funny in all of this mess, she could finally admit to herself that she wanted him. Not just a little attracted, not just a silly little crush because he'd given her a home.

No, she *wanted*. Maybe it had to do with that moment last night where she'd thought he was about to kiss her, because he'd never given any inclination of interest before. So surely his reciprocating feelings was her silly fantasy life taking over because a man like Noah… Well, he knew what he wanted. In all things. If he wanted her, he would've said something.

Probably. Unless there was some noble reason in his head he thought he shouldn't. There was no reason to wish for that. Except, she *wanted*.

She had to push all these thoughts and feelings away, though, because right now Noah was standing there, frowning at her. And she was going to protect him and take care of him right back, so that meant not irritating him.

Which apparently meant the truth.

"There's a text message," she managed to say, reluctantly holding her phone out to him. "From a Boston area code."

"That's where this bastard is?" Noah demanded, his voice hard as he took the phone out of her hands.

Addie nodded. "I don't want to open it. It's always some vile thing." At the spark of Noah's temper moving over his face, she quickly continued. "Whenever he finds me, he texts me threats. This is the first one I've had here. I think he likes making me scared."

Something in him closed up. That anger vanished off his expression, but she could still feel it vibrating under that stoic demeanor. "Some people like knowing they're in your head. That you're running scared. Gives them a thrill."

"Yes," Addie agreed, feeling sick to her stomach. "He could have had Seth by now. So, what he's doing isn't just about getting him back. I mean, I think he wants him back, but he wants me to suffer for as long as possible. I think. I don't know. He doesn't make any sense. That's why I have to run." She wanted to sink to the floor, but she leaned against the wall and it held her up.

"You're done running," Noah said force-fully, as if it was his decision to make. "Now we go after him."

NOAH ANGRILY PUSHED a button on the phone. Though he heard Addie's intake of breath, his anger was too close to a boiling point to worry about comforting her. Besides, he wasn't any good at comforting. He had learned how to protect, and that's what he would keep doing.

He read the text message grimly.

Hello, Addie. Wyoming. Really? Going to ride a few cowboys? Are you about to get lassoed? Maybe we'll have ourselves a little standoff. You, me and the baby. Who will live? Only time will tell.

He hit a few buttons, finding a way to for-ward the text message to Laurel with the num-ber on it. Then he deleted it from Addie's phone, since he didn't want her looking at it.

"Has *he* ever come after you? Or is it al-ways his goons?"

"Uh, goons, as far as I know. Usually only one per town."

Noah nodded. "We'll need to get him here, then."

"Noah, he *killed* my sister. Well, he had her killed. If he comes here, he will have more people killed. Not just me or Seth, but you and your family. He's capable, if he wants to be."

"You don't know how deeply sorry I am about that, Addie. Sorry you had to go through it, sorry someone lost their life. But if you run away, it doesn't end. As long as he has something to come after, he's coming after you. Stopping him is the only answer."

"What if we can't?" There wasn't just a bleak fatality in her tone, there was genuine question.

"I have stopped bad men before. I am not afraid to do it again. We have good and right on our side."

"Good doesn't always win."

"It will here." Because he'd made a promise to himself, growing up in the midst of all that *bad*, that he would make sure good prevailed once he had the power. "Now, instead of arguing, let's discuss our plan."

Addie pushed her fingers to her temples and he took stock of how much sleep had helped her. She wasn't shaking and didn't look as pale. While there were still faint smudges under her eyes, they weren't that deep, concerning black they had been early this morning when they'd arrived at the cabin.

She was more mussed than usual, but that didn't detract from how pretty she looked in the middle of the dim cabin. Like a source of light all herself.

Get yourself together.

She dropped her hands from her temples. "Before we plan, you need to sleep. I don't know what time it is, but I—"

"I caught a few hours once Seth settled," he said, nodding toward the portable crib they'd brought. "I'm fine."

She stared up at him, much the way she'd been doing since he'd told her she was under his protection. Not as if she didn't believe him, but as if he were some mythical creature.

He wanted to be able to be that. Someone she could trust and believe in. Someone who could save her from this. He only prayed he could be.

"Are you hungry? Let me make breakfast. Or dinner. Or whatever meal. I'll make something. That'll be the first step."

"Addie." He gently closed his fingers around her arm as she passed. "You're not the housekeeper here, okay? You don't have to cook or clean."

She looked at his fingers on her arm, then slowly up at him. "If I'm not the housekeeper here, what am I?"

Mine. That stupid word that kept popping unbidden into his head. She stepped closer to him then, like last night, when he'd thought he could kiss her and it would be okay. When he'd been driven by relief instead of reason.

She reached up with her arm not in his grasp. He should let her go. He didn't. She touched his jaw as she had last night, her fingertips lightly brushing across his beard.

Her tongue darted out, licking her bottom lip, and oh, hell.

"You *were* going to kiss me last night before Ty came in," she said on a whisper. A certain, declaratory whisper. "Right?" she added, and if he wasn't totally mistaken, there was *hope* in that "right?"

He might have been able to put her off if not for the hint of vulnerability. Because what was hope but a soft spot people could hurt and break? He cleared his throat, uncomfortable with the directness of the question. "I was thinking about it."

"So, you could do it now."

His gaze dropped to her mouth, no matter how much his conscience told him not to give in to this. Protecting was not taking advantage of. Fighting evil with good was not giving in to something he didn't have any right to want.

But she was close, the darker ring of blue around her pupils visible. The hope in her eyes too tempting. Her lips full and wet from where she'd licked them.

It didn't have to be a distraction. It didn't *have* to be wrong. It could be the start of something.

What? What are you going to start on this *foundation? What do* you *have to offer?*

Since the last question sounded a little bit too much like his father, he pushed it away. He wouldn't be driven by his father's voice.

He leaned closer, watching in fascination as her breath caught, and then she, too, leaned forward.

His phone trilled, which startled him back to reality. They were in a serious, dangerous situation with her child sleeping a few feet away. She was scared and out of sorts.

Now was not the time for nonsense. He glanced at the caller ID, frowned when it was Laurel's number. "It's Laurel."

Addie nodded.

"What?" Noah greeted.

"Bad news," Laurel said in her no-nonsense cop tone. "He's gone."

Before Noah could demand to know what that meant, Laurel continued.

"We did some questioning, but two armed men broke into the station. We're small and understaffed and… Well, three deputies were injured. Badly. They're…" She paused, and though she kept talking in that same efficient cop tone, Noah could tell she was shaken.

"Are you okay?"

"I'd gone to get dinner for everyone," Laurel said bitterly. "Hart got the worst of it. He's in surgery. The other two should be okay, but it'll be… Well, anyway, I need you to be on guard. Three men, at least, are now on the loose and likely after Addie and Seth. I've called in more men, but we don't have an endless supply of deputies."

"We're boarded up. Armed. You keep your men."

"There could be more of them."

Noah tried not to swear. "I'll be ready."

"Everyone in Bent has been told to be on the lookout for out-of-towners and immediately report it to us. Aside from Carsons and

Delaneys, no one has the full story—I didn't want anyone doing anything stupid. So you'll have warning if someone's coming your way, but I'm stretched so thin now here and—"

"I'll handle it."

"We'll all work together to handle it." She paused again. "You know, my brother—"

"No Delaneys."

She sighed heavily. "Addie *is* a Delaney, moron. We're all in this together. If you dare bring up the feud right now, I swear to God…" Then she laughed. "Oh, you did that on purpose to get me riled up about something else."

"I don't know what you're talking about," he muttered. Except she'd sounded *sad*, and sad wasn't going to do anyone any good. "I gotta go."

"Keep your phone on you, and be careful."

"Uh-huh. Keep me updated."

"Will do."

Noah hit End and looked at Addie, who'd moved into the kitchen, her back to him, as she hugged herself. He wasn't sure how much she'd heard, but clearly enough to be concerned. He could try to put it lightly, but he thought after the whole almost-kiss thing, they needed the straightforward truth. "He escaped."

Addie leaned against the tiny slab of countertop in the minimalist kitchen. "How?" she asked, her voice strangled.

Noah didn't want to tell her. He even toyed with the idea of lying to her. But in the end, he couldn't. If they were going to win this, they needed to be open and honest with each other.

"Someone helped him. A few deputies were hurt in the process."

She whirled on him then, all anger and frustration. "I can't have this, Noah. I cannot have people's lives on my head."

"They're on the mob's head. Beginning and end of that story."

She shook her head and marched over to the living room, purposefully keeping as much room between them as possible in the tiny cabin. "I'm packing Seth up and we're running. You can't stop me."

She paused over Seth's crib, clearly warring over the idea of picking him up when he was sleeping.

Noah parked himself in front of the door, picking up the rifle he'd rested there. "You're not going anywhere."

She glanced back at him, her expression going mutinous. "You can't keep me prisoner here."

"Watch me."

Chapter Eight

Addie was so furious she considered walking right up to him and punching him in the gut.

Except Noah was so big and hard her little fist couldn't do much damage, if any. And that was the thing that had dogged her for a year.

She had no strength and no power. She couldn't win this fight. She could only put it off a little while.

And everyone trying to help her was going to die.

Her knees gave out and she fell with an audible *thump* onto the couch, guilt and uselessness washing over her.

"Don't... Don't cry. Please." Noah grumbled.

Which was the first time she realized she *was* crying. Not little slipped-out tears. Huge, fat tears. She sobbed once, tired and overwhelmed. It was easier when it was her and

Seth against the world. She didn't have to deal in hope or guilt. All she had was *run*.

"Addie, honey, come on." She felt the couch depress and Noah's arm go around her shaking shoulders. "Please. Please stop crying. You're not a prisoner. You're just… We're just lying low, that's all. Together. Hell, you have to stop crying. It just about kills me."

He sounded so desperate, she wished she could stop. But she was just so *tired*, and the truth was she wanted to let Noah handle it. Believe him. But the man who'd tried to steal Seth away had escaped, and people had been hurt, and all those people would have been fine if she'd never come here.

"Those men are hurt because of me. You're in this cabin because of me. You should have let me run. I'm only trouble."

His strong arm pulled her tighter. "You're not trouble. You've been a victim, and you've been brave and strong for a long time. Let someone take the reins."

"I'm hardly brave. I'm sitting here crying like a baby."

"You escaped a madman for how long?"

She blew out a breath. "But I can't beat him."

"Maybe not alone. Together we will, and

I don't just mean me. You've got Laurel and Grady and everyone. The whole town is with us. That doesn't make what you've managed to do less. Addie, look at him," he said, gesturing toward the crib and Seth. "He's perfect."

"He is."

"You did that."

"No, I didn't." *He's not mine.* The words were on the tip of her tongue, but Noah's rough hand cupped her cheek.

"Promise me you won't try to run off. Promise me you'll trust me on this. We are in this together, until you're both safe."

He was touching her so gently, looking at her so earnestly, asking for a promise she didn't want to give. She even opened her mouth to refuse the promise, but something in the moment reminded her of before.

Noah believed her. From the beginning. Without hesitation. If she had done that with Kelly, maybe everything would be different.

Grief threatened to swamp her, but she couldn't change the past. What she could do was change her future.

Trusting him to help was what she had to do. And maybe anyone who got hurt along the way… She hated to even think it, but it was true.

She would sacrifice a clean conscience for Seth, so if people got hurt, as long as Seth was safe, she couldn't let it matter.

"Okay. Okay." She nodded, even as his hands stayed on her cheek. "I promise we're in this together." No matter what guilt she had to endure. It was for Seth. If she could remember that…

It was hard to remember anything with Noah's big, rough hand on her face. She'd long since stopped crying, but he was still touching her. And he was not a man given to casual touches.

Yet it didn't feel like the other two moments. Those moments that had been interrupted, where everything in her had stilled and yearned. There was some lack of softness on his face.

But unlike those other two moments, this time he did close the distance between them. His mouth touched hers, and for all the ways Noah had *clearly* resisted this moment, there was nothing tentative about it.

He kissed like a man who knew what he was doing. His lips finding hers unerringly, no matter how much beard separated them.

There was nothing she could have done to prepare herself for that wave of feeling. Something so warm and sweet and bright she thought she couldn't name it.

But the word *hope* whispered across the edges of her consciousness as she reached out for him, wanting to hold on to something. Wanting it to be him.

When he pulled away, all too quickly in her estimation, he searched her face, relaxing a millimeter, and somehow she understood.

It wasn't a real kiss. It wasn't loss of control because passion so consumed him. "You did that to distract me," she accused. She should be angrier, more hurt, but all she could really be was bone-deep glad he'd done it.

Now she knew how much *more* was worth.

He pressed his mouth together, though she thought maybe under the beard was some kind of amused smile. "Maybe," he rumbled.

She crossed her arms over her chest huffily. "It didn't work."

His mouth quirked that tiny bit. "Yes, it did."

Her heart fluttered at his easy confidence. She didn't understand this man. Gruff and sweet, with so many walls, and yet he could kiss like he'd been born to do it and *knew* what kind of effect he had on her.

She was torn between kissing him again— much deeper and much longer this time— and eliciting more of this almost-smiling, certainly half-teasing man out of him.

But a loud *bang*, something like an explosion outside, had them both jumping. Addie was afraid she'd screamed, but in the end it didn't matter. Noah was on his feet, rifle in his hands, and she had already swept Seth up against her chest.

Noah's mouth was a firm line under his beard. Without a word he took her by the arm and propelled her around the couch. He shoved a narrow table against the wall out of the way, and then as if by magic, pulled up a door in the middle of the floor. An actual door.

"It's a cellar. Cramped and dark, but it can keep you safe if you're quiet. Go down there."

"But what about you?"

"I'll handle it. I promise."

"There could be—"

He slapped his phone into her palm. "Call or text everyone. You stay here and safe and let them come to my rescue, got it?"

Remembering her earlier promise to herself—*anything for Seth*—she swallowed and nodded. She turned to the dark space the pulled-up door allowed and did her best to ignore fear of dark or cramped or not knowing as she felt her way down a shaking length of stairs.

Seth wiggled and fussed against her, but was mostly content when she held him hard and close.

"Good?" Noah asked.

"Peachy," she muttered, and then she was plunged into darkness.

NOAH'S HEART BEAT too hard and too fast, but he focused on keeping his breathing even. He kept his mind on the facts he had.

Someone was outside and trying to get in. Addie and Seth were safe in the cellar if he kept them so. The boarded-up windows made no entrance into the cabin undetectable. *He* had the tactical advantage.

Except he couldn't see who was out there or how many, and though he knew the general vicinity that loud bang had come from, he didn't know exactly what had caused it or what kind of weaponry the undetermined number of men had.

He knew how to fight bad men, but he'd

never had to fight off a possible group of them. He'd have to figure it out. Seth and Addie were counting on him.

The door shook in time with another large bang. And then another. He realized grimly there was also a banging coming from the back of the cabin, so there were at least two of them. Trying to get into the cabin from two different directions.

He needed to create some kind of barrier and he needed to make sure he kept both men—if it was only two—far away from Addie and Seth. He didn't want to leave them alone to draw the men away, but if she called Laurel, there would be help on the way.

Because the cabin had been used as a hideout for the Carson clan for over a century, it had all sorts of hidden places and secret exits. Maybe he could sneak out and pick off whoever was out there. Based on the banging, he had a better idea of where they were than they had of where he was.

It was a chance he'd have to take. He couldn't let them get inside. There would be too many ways he could be cornered, too many ways Seth making noise might give Addie away. And he had to know more about what he was dealing with so he wouldn't be caught unaware.

He strode to the kitchen, gripped the rifle under his arm and gave the refrigerator a jerk. He didn't push it all the way out, in case he needed to hide this little secret passageway quickly. Instead, he yanked the wallboard open and shoved his body through the narrow opening.

There was a crawl space that would lead him outside—one of the sides he hadn't heard banging against. And if he miscalculated, well, he pulled his rifle in front of him. He'd use that to nudge the door open, shoot first and ask questions later. Whatever would keep Addie and Seth safe.

On his hands and knees, pushing the rifle in front of him, he squeezed his too-big body through the too-small space. He nudged the door with the gun, then frowned when it didn't budge.

After a few more nudges—harder and harder each time—he finally got the small door to move, but just enough to see what was blocking it.

Snow. Far too many inches of snow. He pushed the rifle behind him, army-crawled up to the slight opening he'd made and got as close to the crack as possible so he could look out.

The world was white. He couldn't even see trees. Just snow, snow and more snow. On the ground, still falling from the sky, accumulating fast.

The chance of help coming was about as remote as it'd ever be. Even if Addie got through to Laurel or a Carson, it'd take extra time.

Which meant he had to get back inside the cabin. There'd be no trying to lure the men away when he didn't have much hope for quick backup.

He turned and pushed himself through the crawl space after pulling the door to the outside closed. He twisted his body this way and that, getting out behind the refrigerator, trying to come up with a new plan.

He was breathing heavily, but he heard the distinct sound of something. Not pounding anymore.

Footsteps.

He didn't have time to push the refrigerator back in place, because a man dressed in black stepped out from the room Addie had been sleeping in just hours before.

Noah raised his rifle and pulled the trigger without even thinking about where the bullet would hit. The most important thing was stopping him.

The man went down with a loud yowl of pain, but another gunshot rang out in the very next moment. Noah only had the split second to realize it wasn't his own gun before a pain so bright and fierce knocked him to his back. His vision dimmed, and damnation, the pain threatened to swallow him whole.

He stared up at the ceiling, a blackness creeping over him, but he fought it off, clinging to consciousness with everything he had in him.

He had to keep Addie safe.

He tried to move, to do anything, but he felt paralyzed. Nothing in his body worked or moved. It only throbbed with fire and ice. How was it both? Searing licks of heat, needling lances of cold.

When a man stood over him, hooded and dim himself, it gave Noah something external to focus on. The man's black coat, not fit for a Wyoming winter, was covered in melted snow droplets. He had his face covered by a bandanna or hat. His eyes were a flat brown.

Evil eyes that were familiar—not because he knew this man, but because Noah had stared evil in the face before.

"Where's the baby?" the man rasped, pointing his small handgun at Noah's head.

Noah groaned, more for show, though the pain in his side was a blinding, searing fire. He'd heard Addie scream, but apparently the man hadn't, or just couldn't figure out where they were.

Noah thought of Addie and Seth and pretended to roll his eyes back in his head. He could hear Seth crying now, which distracted the man's attention. Noah took that brief moment to gather all his strength and kick as hard and groin-targeted as he could.

Chapter Nine

Addie listened to the persistent thumping. She knew it was people trying to get in. People trying to get her and Seth.

She knew Noah would fight them with all he had, but would it be enough? The horrifying worry that he was only one man and there were at least two men out there curdled her stomach.

She reminded herself she'd texted every last Carson and Delaney Noah had in his phone. Even though she hadn't had a response, the messages showed as sent, which meant she only needed one person to see it.

She could not think about what it might mean if no one was looking at their phone. If no one came to help them. So she paced the cellar, trying to work off all her nerves while at the same time keeping Seth happy. She needed to feed him. Even if Noah had fed him while she'd been asleep, he'd be getting hungry again.

She glanced above at the light footsteps. She knew Noah was moving around carefully and quietly on purpose and *God* she just could not think about what he was doing up there.

She used the weak light from Noah's tiny phone screen to illuminate her surroundings until she found a large flashlight sitting at the base of the stairs. She clicked it on, relief coursing through her when a strong beam popped out.

Clearly the Carsons used this cabin at least somewhat frequently, because there were a few shelves lined with provisions. Mainly canned foods, but if she could find one with a pop-top, she could at least give Seth a little something to keep him happy.

No matter that her arms shook and she felt sick to her stomach, she forced herself to read through all the labels. She found a can of pears, one of Seth's favorites.

"Okay, little man, let's get you a snack." She looked around the cellar again with Noah's flashlight. She needed a blanket or something she could put Seth on.

She poked around a pile of old furniture in the corner. Broken chairs, a bent mattress frame. Tools of some sort. A conglomeration of rusty, broken crap.

And a crib. She blinked at it. The legs had been broken off of it, and there was no mattress, but it had once been a crib.

"Something is going our way, Seth," she murmured, glancing warily above her as things got eerily quiet.

Quiet was good. Quiet had to be good.

Balancing Seth on her hip, she carefully picked through the debris of nonsense and pulled the crib out. She studied it, then the room around her. If it was even, and she could push the broken side up against a wall, it could act as an effective playpen if she wanted to go check on Noah.

She heard footsteps again, tried not to think too hard about what that silence might have meant.

She shrugged out of her sweater and placed it in the bottom of the crib. Quickly she ran her fingers around the wood and didn't find any exposed nails or sharp edges. She set Seth down and searched around for other soft things.

She found a stack of folded dish towels and sniffed them gingerly. A little musty, but not terrible. She started placing them over the corners of the crib. A little softening to—

The gunshot was so loud, so close, she screamed. Seth began to wail and she grabbed him to her chest, trying to muffle both their cries as another gunshot almost immediately rang out.

Two gunshots was not good. She didn't have a weapon, but she did have this pile of tools. She bounced Seth until he stopped crying, and she tried to keep her own tears at bay as she heard another thump, then more thumps. Grunts.

No gunshots.

She scrambled to the pile of debris and grabbed the heaviest, sharpest-looking tool she could find. She'd pushed the crib against the wall sort of behind the stairs, and that would work in her favor if she could keep Seth quiet.

The food. The food. She set the tool down by the crib and grabbed the can she'd dropped. She transferred Seth to the little crib and made silly faces to keep him distracted and quiet as she opened the can.

Seth gurgled out a laugh at one of her faces, but it didn't assuage any of her shaking fear, because something scraped against the floor right above her. She could hear someone fiddling with the floorboard. Oh, God, it wasn't Noah. Noah knew how to open it.

On a strangled sob she popped the can of pears open and grabbed one without thinking twice. She handed it to Seth. Usually she didn't give him such big pieces, but she needed time. She needed to keep them both safe.

She clicked off the flashlight just as the door opened and light shone in. Addie grabbed the tool and gripped it in both hands as she stepped back into the shadows.

The tool was sharp. It would cause serious damage even with her limited strength. Her stomach threatened to revolt, but she refused to let it.

She was done running, cowering and giving in. She'd made that choice to stand and fight up there with Noah. So she would do whatever it took. Whatever it took to fight for him. Fight for Seth.

She was done being a victim.

She swallowed the bile that threatened to escape her throat as some man who was most definitely not Noah took the stairs. He didn't have a flashlight, which put her at an advantage. Seth was liable to make a noise any second, so she had to be ready.

She quietly lifted the tool above her head and just as Seth murmured happily over a piece of pear, the man turned.

She brought the tool down onto his skull as hard as she could, and he strangled out a scream and fell in a heap. Her stomach lurched as she realized the tool was lodged in his skull as it fell with him.

But she couldn't worry about her stomach. She needed to get to Noah, and if no one was coming at the sound of the man's scream, he had to be acting alone.

Or someone else is hurting Noah.

She picked Seth up, much to his screaming dismay, and scurried around the motionless body on the floor.

Oh, God, had she killed him?

Had *he* killed Noah?

She climbed the stairs, Seth screaming in her ear. She stumbled up into the living room, desperately searching for Noah.

Then she saw him lying on the floor. And blood. Too much blood.

"Noah. Noah." She dropped to her knees next to him, not even worried she was getting bloody herself as long as she kept Seth out of it. "Noah. You have to be alive, Noah."

"No! No!" Seth said gleefully, clearly not understanding the scene around them.

Addie had to focus. Focus on what was in front of her. He'd clearly been shot. Blood pooled on one side of his body, but not the other. His face was ashen. But, oh, *God*, his chest was moving. Up and down.

"Noah." She wasn't sure what to do with a gunshot wound. Pressure. That's what they did in the movies, right? Apply pressure.

"Not dead," he muttered, though his eyes stayed closed.

"Oh, thank God you're awake." She pressed a kiss to his forehead and his eyelids fluttered, but they didn't fully open.

"No!" Seth squealed again.

"Where's he?" Noah demanded.

She assumed he meant the man she'd... "I... Well, he came down and I think I killed him." She'd still need to close up the door, cover it with something really heavy to keep him down there just in case. But for now she had to focus on Noah.

"Good," Noah replied, his voice firm for the first time, though his eyes remained closed. "I killed the other one. Must be it or they'd be in here."

"For now."

Noah grunted.

"I have to… I have to get you help." She pawed at her pocket for the phone Noah had given her earlier. She had a text from Laurel and as she clicked to read it, Noah said almost the exact thing.

Blizzard. Can't get up. Grady and Ty trying with horses. Will be a while.

"Blizzard. No help."

Addie closed her eyes in an effort to try to think. "We need to focus on you right now." She stood and crossed to the travel crib. It was upended, but she righted it and set Seth inside, cooing sweet reassurances at him as she gave him a toy.

She went through the next few steps as though it were a to-do list. Get as many blankets, towels and washcloths she could. Put a pillow under Noah's head. Peel the bloodied shirt away from his side. Try not to throw up. Gently wash out the terrible wound.

Noah hissed out a breath, but that just reassured her he was *alive*. "Is there a first aid kit anywhere?"

"Bathroom maybe," he muttered.

She was on her feet in an instant. Seth

fussed but not a full-blown cry…yet. She had
to get Noah some semblance of patched up.
She wished she could move him to a bed, but
who would lift him? Her and what army?

She jerked open the cabinet under the sink
and rummaged. Soap, extra toilet paper, a box
of condoms. Her cheeks warmed, but she kept
looking until she found a flimsy canvas pouch
with the red first aid cross on it.

She hastened back to Noah's side. His eyes
were open so she tried to smile down at him.
"Well, we survived."

His mouth didn't move and he looked so
pale even under all his hair and beard. "For
now," he managed in the same tone of voice
she'd used earlier.

Wasn't that the truth?

She studied the wound again, and it was
bleeding once more. She tried not to let de-
spair wash over her. The only way Noah survived this was her somehow making it so.

So that's what she'd have to do.

IT WAS A strange thing to be shot. Noah would
have thought just the bleeding part of his body
would hurt, but everything hurt. He kept losing consciousness, awakening who knew how
long later on the cold, uncomfortable floor.

He tried not to groan as he forced his eyes open. He looked around the quiet room. The only sound he recognized was Seth sucking on a bottle.

It was a little bit of a relief to know things were business as usual for the baby.

Addie appeared in his wavering vision, and she knelt next to him, a tremulous smile on her face. "Oh, good, you're really awake this time."

"Was I kind of awake before?"

She nodded down at his chest and he realized that under the blanket draped over him he was shirtless and bandaged. "You came to a few times when I was bandaging you up best as I could. Well, I called Laurel and she patched me through to a paramedic. You're lucky because it didn't seem to make any kind of…hole."

No, the bullet seemed to have grazed him. Badly, but no holes and no bullets floundering around in his body. It was good and it was lucky.

He was having trouble feeling it.

"I need to get up," he said. Lying there was making things worse. If he got up and moved around he could hold on to consciousness. He tried to push himself into a sitting position.

His head swam, his stomach roiled and the pain in his side *burned.* Addie's arms came around him, though, surprisingly sturdy, and she held him up.

He was so damn dizzy, even if he had the strength he wasn't sure he could get to his feet. It was unacceptable. This was all unacceptable. Because he did need stitches, and there was no way to get them. Which meant he was going to halfway bleed to death and be a weak, useless liability to Addie and Seth.

No, he wouldn't be that.

"We need to secure the place. They got in through your room—"

"I dragged the man you shot outside," Addie said flatly. "I boarded up the bedroom window again best as I could. I've locked the room from the outside—since we won't be spending any more time in separate rooms, we don't need it. I also barricaded the cellar just in case the man I…hurt isn't dead."

He stared. "You did *all* that while I was out?"

"It's much better than sitting here fretting that you're dead. Or waiting. Grady and Ty are still trying to get to us with the horses, but the blizzard set them back quite a bit. Apparently Ty knows some battlefield medicine or *something* and can stitch you up when he gets here." Addie shuddered.

"I don't know what to say." Or feel. Or do. She'd handled it all. He was a burden now, but somehow she'd handled it all.

"Let's get you to bed and then you're going to lie down and stay put. You need to rest and not aggravate the bleeding until someone can get up here to help." She glanced over at Seth's travel crib. "Let's do it now before he finishes that bottle and starts yelling."

He wasn't sure he could get to his feet, but he wasn't about to admit that to her. There had to be *something* he could handle. Something he could do.

He rolled to the side that wasn't injured and tried desperately not to groan or moan as he struggled onto his feet. The world tipped, swayed, but he closed his eyes and with Addie's arms around him, he managed to stay upright.

Because slight little Addie—the woman he'd deemed fragile the first time he'd met her—held him up as he swayed.

She pulled the blankets that had been around him over his shoulders, then held tight, leaning her body against his tipping one as he took a step.

He walked, and noted she moved slower than he might have tried to. She was holding him back. Making him take it easy. He should have worked up some irritation, but mostly he could only concentrate on getting the interminable distance from the kitchen floor to his bed.

But they inched their way there, no matter how awful he felt. Somehow he got his feet to keep moving forward. Managed to ease himself onto his bed, with Addie's help.

Once he was prone again, he managed a full, painful breath. She was already tucking blankets around him, though she paused to inspect the bandage, the strands of her hair drifting across his chest. Somewhere deep down there was the slightest flutter of enjoyment and he figured he had a chance of surviving this yet.

"You need to rest. No getting up without help. No pushing yourself. Do you understand me?"

He grunted irritably. He hoped she considered it assent, even though it wasn't. Not a promise, because why would he promise that?

"You need to try to get something to eat. Keep up your strength. I'm going to—"

He grabbed her, unmanned at the fact there

was a beat of panic at the thought of her leaving him. It was the aftereffect of shock. Had to be.

She patted his hand reassuringly, and it was that something like *pity* in her gaze that had him withdrawing his hand. He wasn't to be pitied. Yeah, he'd been shot trying to save *her*.

And she saved herself, didn't she?

"I'm just going to get Seth. Grab you some soup I already warmed up. Trust me, Noah, the three of us are plastered to one another's sides until this is all over."

She slid off the bed, and still that panic inside him didn't disappear. "How'd you kill him without a gun?" he asked. Anything to keep her here. Here where he could see her. Where he could assure himself they'd come out this on the other side.

For now. What about the next other side?

Addie fiddled with the collar of her T-shirt, eyes darting this way and that. "Well." She cleared her throat. "Th-there were a bunch of tools down there so I just picked up the sharpest, biggest one and when he came down the stairs I hid in the shadows, then bashed him over the head." She let out a shaky breath. "I've never…hurt someone. I've never had to. I don't know how to feel."

"You feel relieved you were able to defend yourself," he said, hoping even though he felt weak and shaky and a million other unacceptable things she could feel that in her bones. "You took the relief of saving yourself or someone else—it was all you could do." He should know.

She cocked her head, those blue eyes studying him. He might have fidgeted if he'd had the energy. "You've hurt people? I mean, besides today?" she asked on a whisper.

Part of him wanted to lie or hedge, but he was too tired, too beat down to do either. "When I've had to."

"Like when?"

"It isn't important now. What's important is surviving until Grady and Ty get here. What's important is coming up with the next step of our plan."

"What on earth is the next step going to be?"

The trouble was, he didn't know.

Chapter Ten

Watching Noah search for an answer to that question hurt almost as much as watching him suffer through what must be unbearable pain. Even though the paramedic she'd talked to who'd walked her through sterilizing and bandaging Noah's wound had assured her that Noah would survive for days as long as he rested and kept hydrated, Noah looked terrible. From his ashen complexion to the way he winced at every move.

Seth began to fuss in the main room and she forced herself to smile at Noah. "Be right back."

She wasn't sure if it was fear or something else written all over his face. He clearly didn't want her to leave, but she had to get Seth and try to feed Noah.

It was strange, and maybe a little warped, but knowing Noah was hurt calmed her somehow. Much like protecting Seth, it gave her a purpose. She couldn't cry. She couldn't fall apart. She had to be strong for her men.

Noah is not your man.

Well, she could pretend he was. It might get her through this whole nightmare, and that was the goal. Coming out on the other side.

She moved into the living room and smiled at Seth. He made angry noises, though hadn't gone into full-blown tantrum yet. He'd been up for a solid eight hours now, and was fighting a nap like a champ. But he was otherwise unaffected by everything that had happened, and she could only be grateful for that. It soothed.

She picked up the toy he'd thrown out of his travel crib and handed it to him. He took it, though he didn't smile. When she picked him up, he sighed a little and nuzzled into her shoulder.

Oh, he was getting so big. And somehow she had to make sure he grew up. When she stepped into the room, she laid Seth in the middle of the bed next to Noah.

He fussed, then rolled to his side, cuddling up with Noah's not-shot side.

Noah looked slightly alarmed, but Addie didn't have time to assure him Seth would be okay for a few minutes. She went back and folded the travel crib, then set it back up in the room before heading to the kitchen.

She ladled out some soup she'd been keeping warm for when Noah woke up. She went through the very normal motions of making Noah dinner, then went through the not-so-normal motions of taking it to him.

In bed.

With a sleeping baby between you and a gaping wound from a bullet in his side and who knows how many psychopaths after you.

She darted a look at the door, the many locks, then the windows and all the boarding up they'd done. She'd found a heavy metal cabinet in a back mudroom and moved it over the door to the cellar. None of these things would permanently keep bad people out, but it would slow them down and give her and Noah warning.

Besides, she had the snow in her favor now. Unless there'd been other men with the two they'd killed who were lying in wait, any more of Peter's men would have to contend with the same weather Grady and Ty were facing.

She straightened her shoulders and breezed

back into Noah's room, hoping she looked far more calm and capable than she felt.

She lost some of that facade, though, when she caught sight of the big, bearded cowboy with his arm delicately placed around the fast-asleep baby. Something very nearly *panged* inside her, but she couldn't allow herself to dwell on any pangs.

"You need to try to eat as much of this as you can," she said quietly. She placed the bowl of soup on the sturdy, no-nonsense nightstand. "I'll go get a chair," she said, searching the room. "Then I can feed you."

"No."

"Noah—"

"Just need to sit up, and I can do it myself," he said through clenched teeth as he worked to move himself into a sitting position, pain etched all over his face.

She stood over him, fisting her hands on her hips. "You shouldn't. Don't make me stop you from moving."

He winged up an eyebrow at her, and something in that dark expression had her faltering a little bit. Because it made her think of other things she shouldn't be thinking of with Seth asleep next to him and the gaping wound in Noah's side.

"You're not feeding me," he said resolutely as he struggled to get into a sitting position in the bed.

She wanted to push him back down, but she was afraid she'd only hurt him more, so she tried to take a different approach. "It wouldn't be any problem to do it. You're injured. Let me take care of—"

"You're not feeding me," he repeated.

Maybe she was reaching, but his complexion didn't seem quite as gray, even as he managed to lean against the wall…because in this sparse, no-nonsense room there was no headboard.

She frowned at him, then at the soup, then back at him. "Fine. You've worn me down. Let it cool while I move Seth to—"

"He's fine. Give me the soup."

"Noah."

"Addie, you killed a man. Saved us. Boarded up windows and talked to paramedics. Give me the soup and take a sit."

You killed a man. She was trying so very hard not to contemplate that. So she handed him his soup.

"What part of take a sit did you not understand?" Noah asked, and though his tone was mild she didn't miss the harsh thread of steel in his tone.

"What part of *I killed a man* don't you understand? I might snap and kill you, too, if you keep bossing me around."

Noah smiled then. Actually smiled. "I'll take my chances."

"I want to be relieved you're feeling good enough to smile, except you so rarely smile, I'm just prone to think you have a fever or some kind of horrible brain sickness."

"If I do, you should probably sit down because your fluttering around is stressing me out."

Addie frowned. "I'm not... I don't *flutter.*" This time he didn't smile, but his lips *did* quirk upward. She slid onto the bed, Seth's sleeping body between them. She sighed heavily. "If I sit still, all I think about is all the ways things can go wrong."

He reached over and touched her arm, just a gentle brush of fingertips. "We'll get through this."

Addie blew out a breath. "We're stuck in a room in a tiny cabin that people have already infiltrated in the middle of a blizzard with no medical help or backup."

"But we fought off two armed men."

She frowned. "You've been *shot*, that's not exactly a victory."

"Not dead, though." He gave her arm a little squeeze, and though he tried to hide it, she noticed the wince. "Why don't you try to sleep while I eat? We need to take the opportunities to rest while we can."

"Noah…" Only she didn't know what to say or ask. She glanced down at Seth, who was sprawled out between them, blissfully unaware of everything going on around him.

She had to make sure he stayed that way, and this ended. "Noah, when you said you'd hurt people before this because you'd had to, what did you mean?"

He opened his mouth, most definitely to change the subject, but she needed to know. Needed to know how to go on from here. How to deal with the fact she'd hurt someone. "Tell me."

NOAH BROUGHT THE spoon to his mouth, slowly, carefully. Not because his body hurt, though it did, but because every part of him recoiled at the idea of telling her that. It would likely change her opinion of him, and more than that, he didn't want to tear down all those walls that kept it firmly in the past.

But maybe she needed to hear it. She needed to understand how to justify it so she could accept the things a person had to do to keep the people she loved safe.

She was so tense, sitting there on the opposite side of his bed. Eyes darting everywhere, hands clasping and unclasping. It was an interesting dichotomy: the woman who'd managed to do *everything* while he'd been unconscious, and this nervous, afraid-to-sit-and-think woman sharing a bed with him.

With a baby between you, idiot.

"My father wasn't a particularly kind man." Understatement of the year. "Ty and I were capable of withstanding that, but sometimes his targets weren't quite as fair or equal to the task."

"I'm not sure a son should ever have to be equal to the task of an unkind father."

"It was fine. We were fine, but Vanessa came to live with us for a bit when she was in high school. Her dad had died, and she'd gotten kicked out of her mother's house when her mother's new husband hadn't treated her so well. It was the only place to go, and we figured we'd keep her safe."

"From what? Unkindness? Because *safe* sounds like more than an unkind father."

"I suppose it was. It most certainly was when it came to Vanessa. Dad drank, more once Mom was gone, and she was by this point. Once Dad decided someone had the devil in them…"

"What does that even mean?"

Noah shrugged, trying not to think too deeply on it. Trying not to remember it as viscerally as he usually did, but it was a bit too much. Seth and Addie. This cabin. The pain throbbing at his side.

He took another spoonful of the soup, trying to will all this old ugliness away with the slide of warm soup down his throat. It didn't work. Instead the black cloud swirled around him like its own thick, heavy being.

But Addie slid her hand over his forearm. Gentle and sweet, and the black cloud didn't depart, but that heaviness lifted.

"He was a hard man. A vicious man. Made worse when he was drinking. He decided Vanessa had the devil in her and it was his job to get it out. I never quite understood it. He was not a religious man. No paragon of virtue. A Carson villain as much as any that came before."

"So you hurt him to protect Vanessa?"

Noah shouldn't have been surprised Addie

could put it together, though it shamed him some. It must be obvious, the mark his father had made on him no matter how many years he'd striven to do good, *be* good.

"I guess."

"You *guess*?"

"I mean, that's the general gist."

"Then what's the actual story? I don't just want the gist."

He glanced at her then, the frown on her face, the line dug across her forehead. He didn't quite understand this woman, though he supposed he'd very purposefully tried *not* to understand her. To keep his distance. To keep everyone safely at arm's length.

But she'd slid under that at some point, and he didn't think she'd even really tried. She'd shown up at his door looking fragile and terrified, and he'd been certain it would be easy or she'd disappear or something.

She'd killed a man. In self-defense. Of herself, her son, of *him*. And her hand rested on his arm, a featherlight touch, soft and sweet.

But she was stronger than all that. It was probably the blood loss, but he wanted to tell her now.

"Sometimes he'd whale on us," Noah offered, lifting a shoulder. "We were big enough to take it. Vanessa wasn't. I couldn't let him hurt her. Not just because she was my cousin and family, but because she hadn't done anything wrong. She didn't deserve it."

"Then neither did you or Ty."

But they'd weathered their father's many storms and Noah had never felt... It had felt like his lot in life. The way things were. He wasn't a philosophical man. He'd always played the cards he'd been dealt. Bitterness didn't save anyone.

But violence could. "He went after her one day. Really went after her." Noah tried to block it out. The sound of Vanessa sobbing, how close his father had come to hurting her. In every way possible.

"I wanted to kill him. To end it. Part of me wanted that." Still, even years after Dad had died in a cell somewhere. He wished he'd killed him himself.

"And that weighs on you," Addie said, as if she couldn't understand why even though it was obvious.

"He was my father. Everything he was weighs on me."

"But you're you." Her hand slid up his arm to cup his cheek. She even smiled. How could she possibly smile at *that*? "A good man. A noble one. I didn't think they existed, Noah. Not outside of fairy tales."

"I'm no fairy tale."

Sheer amusement flashed in her eyes, and it sent a pang of longing through him he wasn't sure he'd ever understand.

"No. You're no fairy tale, but you remind me good exists in the real world when I most need to remember that." She leaned across the sleeping baby and gently brushed her mouth across his bearded cheek. "Thank you," she whispered.

Maybe if they weren't on the run, if she hadn't killed a man, if he wasn't bleeding profusely where a man had shot him, he might have known what to do with all that. As it was, all he could do was stare.

"You should rest," he managed to say, his voice rusty and pained.

She sighed, dropping her hand from his cheek and settling into the pillows underneath her head. She stared at the ceiling rather than him. "So should you."

"Food first for me, which means you rest first. Just take a little nap while Seth does, huh?"

She yawned, snuggling deeper into the pillows. "Mmm. Maybe." She turned her gaze to him, so solemn and serious. "Noah…"

"We're going to make it out of here. I promise." If he of all people could make her believe in good, he could get her out of here. He would.

"No, it isn't that. It's just… Seth's not—"

A loud pounding reverberated through the cabin. Noah bit back a curse as he tried to jump into action and the move caused a screaming burn in his side. He put a hand on Addie's arm as he glanced at her pale face.

Three short raps later and Noah let out a sigh of relief. "It's Ty."

Chapter Eleven

Addie scurried out of the bed and toward the front door, hoping Seth would stay asleep and Noah would stay put.

Even though Noah had seemed so abundantly sure it was Ty at the door, Addie hesitated. What if it was a trick? What if Noah was hallucinating? She frantically searched the living room and kitchen for a weapon. For anything.

Before she could grab a knife from the kitchen, she heard Noah's footsteps and labored breathing. She turned and glared at him.

"You should have stayed in bed."

He didn't say anything, just carefully maneuvered himself to the door. He pounded on it, and it was only then she realized he knew it was Ty because they were pounding in some secret code.

"You could have explained."

Noah merely grunted.

"Move this?"

Addie hurried to move the couch away from the door, Noah reaching out to open the locks on the door as she did.

Irritably, she slapped his hand away and undid the last lock herself before yanking the door open.

Ty stood there, his hat pulled low and the brim dusted with snow. He had to step up and over to get through the snowdrift that had piled up outside the door.

"What the hell are you doing on your feet, idiot?" Ty demanded the moment he stepped inside and his eyes landed on Noah. He quickly started pushing Noah back toward the room he'd only just come from.

"Where's Grady?" Noah said.

"Shoveling out some room for the horses in the barn. We'll search the area once I've got you patched up," Ty returned. With absolutely no preamble he turned to Addie. "Boil water, find me all the bandages or makeshift bandages you can, and a few towels. Bring them to the bed."

"Seth's asleep in the bed," Noah muttered as Ty kept pushing him toward the bedroom.

Without even stopping, Ty barked out another order Addie's way. "Move the kid out of the bed."

"You'll be respectful," Noah said in that stern, no-nonsense tone.

Ty rolled his eyes. "Leave it to you with a bullet hole in your side to worry about respectful."

"It's fine. The most important thing is patching Noah up," Addie said resolutely, passing them both into the room and carefully maneuvering Seth from the bed to the mobile crib.

She stood there for a second looking at her baby as he squirmed, scowled, then fell back to sleep. She'd been so close to telling Noah he wasn't hers, which had been so silly. What did it matter? In every important way, Seth was hers.

No one needed to know that she had no legal claim over him. That would complicate everything.

On a deep breath, she turned to Ty, who was disapprovingly helping Noah into a prone position on the bed.

"Boiling water, bandages, towels. Anything else?"

"That'll do," Ty returned, lifting Noah's makeshift bandages she'd put on him herself. "You're one lucky son of a gun," Ty muttered to his brother, and it was in that moment Addie realized Ty's gruffness and irritation all stemmed from worry and fear.

It softened her some, and steadied her more. This family was like nothing she'd ever known, and she'd do whatever she could to help them, protect them. She just had to remind herself every now and again she didn't really belong to them, no matter what it might feel like when Noah touched her so gently, kissed her to distract her or smiled at her despite the bullet wound in his side.

As Addie marched to the kitchen, Grady came inside. He stomped his snowy boots on the mat as he latched the front door with the variety of locks. He looked pissed and dangerous, and yet it didn't make her nervous or even guilty. It made her glad this man was on her side.

"I saw the dead one outside. Nothing of any interest on him," Grady said roughly as Addie prepared a pot to boil water in. "Laurel said there were two."

"I... There's one in the cellar," Addie said, nodding toward the metal cabinet she'd dragged across the door. "I think... I think he's dead." Dead. She'd killed a man and kept *telling* people about it and she wasn't sure how to feel about it…except Noah had said she should be relieved. Glad she'd protected herself and Seth. *And him.*

"If he's not dead now, he will be," Grady said, so cool and matter-of-fact it sent a shiver of fear through Addie.

Grady pulled a small gun from beneath the jacket he still wore. Whatever stabs of guilt from before the attack were gone now, because she could only be relieved she had people to help her.

Grady moved the cabinet off from the cellar door and eased his way down. Addie grabbed a knife from a drawer and eased her way close to the cellar. While she thought the man was dead, she'd absolutely jump to Grady's defense on the off chance the man was alive and got the better of him.

But Grady returned, grim-faced and serious. "Dead," he said stoically, and yet she could tell he was searching her face for signs of distress.

Addie straightened her shoulders. "Good." She wanted it to be good. She headed back for the kitchen and the boiling water.

"Laurel's beating herself up over this."

"She shouldn't," Addie said resolutely. "They're mobsters. Escaping police custody and doing the most damage possible is part of their job."

She grabbed some towels out of the drawer, trying to force her face to look calm and serious. Like Laurel herself. In charge and ready for anything.

Grady smiled ruefully. "And just think, you and Noah managed to stop a few. I wish I could convince Laurel she's not to blame, but what we feel and what's the truth isn't always the same. Not much we can do about it. Though Laurel will try, till she's blue in the face and keeling over. We're all going to try to put an end to this."

"Noah thinks we need to lure Peter here. I think he'll just keep sending men. After all, we know at least one more is out there. I can only imagine more are coming to do more damage."

"We'll handle it."

"Are all you Carsons so sure of yourselves?"

Grady grinned. "Damn right we are. You don't survive centuries of being on the wrong side of history without knowing how to face the bad guy."

But Peter was so much more than a *bad* guy. Addie thought he was evil incarnate. Even a rational man would have taken Seth long ago. Instead, he wanted her in a constant state of fear. She had no doubt Peter would take away everything she loved before he was done.

She had to find some Carson bravery and surety. She had to believe in her own power, and theirs.

Peter couldn't win this, if she had to sacrifice herself to make sure he didn't.

"Grady, I have a plan." The scariest plan she'd ever considered. Dangerous. Possibly deadly. But if she had to face that to keep everyone she loved safe, well, then so be it.

NOAH WOULD NOT admit to anyone, even his own brother, he was feeling a little woozy. Part the loss of blood, and part the fact that someone stitching him up while he was unmedicated wasn't really that great of a time.

"That should do it," Ty said, and because Noah had spent his childhood shoulder-to-shoulder with his brother and knew all the inflections of his voice, he knew Ty was struggling with all this.

He also knew the last thing Ty would want was to talk about it.

"How often you have to do that in the army?"

"Don't worry about it."

So Ty didn't want to talk about that, either. Well, lucky for Ty Noah didn't have the energy to push. "When am I going to feel normal?"

Ty raised an eyebrow as he cleaned up the mess he'd made. "You got shot and patched up by passable emergency stitches at best. You need a whole hell of a lot of rest. Worry about that, not when."

"I have to keep her safe. *Them* safe."

"You have to rest first."

"I don't have time to rest."

Ty sighed heavily and Seth began to move around. A few little whimpers escaped his mouth, but he was still half-asleep.

"There is too much at stake," Noah said in a whisper. "Don't you see that?"

"Of course I see that. I also see that you've been shot. You're going to have to let some people step up and do the protecting here. We're all on it. Carsons. Delaneys."

"What good has that ever done?"

"You're still alive, aren't you?" Ty returned.

"Thanks to Addie."

"Well, she's a Delaney herself."

Noah scowled, well, much as he could with this terrible exhaustion dogging him. "You're not hearing me."

"I'm hearing you just fine. Enough to know you're getting mixed up with her."

"I'm protecting her," Noah replied resolutely. He was not mixed up in anything, because Addie was…well, whatever she was. *Strong. Vibrant. Everything.*

"Whatever you want to call it," Ty said with a shrug, having cleaned up all the stitching debris. "You need to rest before you can do more of it."

Seth began to whimper in earnest and Ty looked at the baby with something like trepidation in his gaze. "I'll get Addie."

"He won't bite you, you know," Noah offered irritably.

"I'll get Addie," Ty repeated, hurrying out of the room.

"Coward," Noah muttered, smiling over at Seth. "I'd pick you up, but I think I'd get in a little bit of trouble, kid." He painfully adjusted so Seth would be able to see him over the edge of his crib.

"No!" the boy demanded, pounding his little stuffed animal against the sides of the crib.

"I'd be in a whole heap of trouble."

"No," he repeated forcefully, and Noah had to smile. A year old and he already had Addie's spirit. A no-nonsense certainty, but with it a certain headstrong quality that wasn't Addie at all, and still Noah admired it. Because it would serve the boy well as he grew up.

Seth was damn well going to grow up somewhere where Noah could protect him.

"Awake already, baby?" Addie swept in, smiling at Seth as she scooped him into her arms. She turned to Noah. "You okay?"

"I'll live."

"Well, that is encouraging," she returned. Her voice was…odd. A little high. Not exactly panic, but nerves threaded through it. He watched as she moved around the room, collecting Seth's diaper change supplies.

Something was wrong. He'd learned in the past few months that poking at it would only make her insist everything was fine. He had to be sneakier in getting the information out of her.

Too bad he didn't have any idea how to be sneaky.

"Everything okay out there?"

"Oh, you know." Addie's hand fluttered in the air as she laid Seth down on the bed, preparing to change his diaper. "The guy in the cellar is definitely dead. Laurel is blaming herself." She hesitated a second, only a second, before she said the next part. "Grady and I devised a plan."

Noah could tell by hesitation he wouldn't like the plan at all. Besides, why was she devising plans with Grady?

"What kind of plan?" he asked, hoping his voice sounded calm and not accusatory.

She smiled sweetly at him. Too sweetly as she expertly pulled the used diaper off Seth's wriggling body and wiped him up before replacing it with a new diaper.

"You need to rest. We'll catch you all up when you're feeling a little more up to things." She finished changing Seth's diaper and pulled the boy to his feet, tugging his pants back up.

"Catch me up now."

"Everything is fi—"

When he started to get up, she hurried to his side of the bed, Seth bouncing happily on her hip. She slid onto the bed next to him, pressing him back into the pillow. Not forcefully enough that he *had* to lie back down, but he didn't like the idea of fighting her. Not when she was touching him and looking at him with such concern in her expression.

"Don't get up." She didn't say it forcefully like Ty had, but plaintively, worry and hurt swirling in her blue eyes. He didn't want to admit it might come from the same place—care.

"No!" Seth grabbed Noah's nose. Hard. And squealed for effect.

Addie gently pried Seth's fingers off his face. "You need to rest."

"Now is not the time to rest. I can rest when this is over."

"Ty's worried. I can tell he's worried. Can't you be a good patient? For your brother?"

Noah grunted.

"I'll take that as a yes." Addie smiled. "I'm going to go get Seth something to eat. Why don't you try to rest?"

"No! No! No!" Seth lunged at him, smacking his pudgy hands against Noah's cheek.

"Gentle," Addie said soothingly.

It was all too much, these two people who'd come to mean so much to him no matter how hard he'd tried to keep them out. He'd told Addie the worst parts of himself, and she was still here, wanting to protect him and get him better. That little boy *knew* him and *liked* him for whatever darn reason.

He had to protect them, not just because it was the right thing to do, but because he cared. He needed them, much to his own dismay and fear.

But dismay and fear were no match for determination. He took Addie's free hand, gave it a squeeze as her blue gaze whipped to his, looking surprised by the initiation of physical contact.

Which was a little much. He had kissed her before everything had blown up. Maybe he'd used the distraction excuse, but that didn't mean...

Well, none of it meant anything until she and Seth were safe. "Tell me what the plan is, Addie. I care too much about you to pretend I'm not worried about this."

She blinked, clearly taken aback by the mention of care, and maybe he should have been embarrassed or taken the words back, but he was too tired. Too tired to pretend, to keep it all locked down.

"You won't like it, Noah. I'm sorry. But you have to understand, it's what I have to do. For Seth. Once and for all."

"Explain," he growled.

"I'm going to be bait."

"Over my dead—"

"It'll get Peter here, and if we plan it out right, Laurel will have grounds to arrest him and transfer him to the FBI, which means he won't be able to escape this time."

"You don't know that."

He could tell that doubt hurt her, scared her, but she clearly needed both so she'd start thinking clearly.

"Or maybe I kill him, Noah. Maybe I do that. I don't know. What I do know is I can't keep running. You said so yourself. He has to come here. He doesn't want Seth, not really. He wants to cause me pain. So, I give him the chance."

"We can make that happen without you being bait."

"Yes, it's gone so well so far," she said drily, pointing to his bandaged side.

Which poked at his pride as much as the fear settling in his gut. That she would put herself in a situation where she could be hurt, or worse.

"I won't allow it."

She scoffed, shoving to her feet. Seth complained in his baby gibberish but Addie only paced. "I don't know why you insist on acting as though you have any say, any right. You don't get to tell me how to live my life, Noah Carson. You don't get to boss me around. This is my problem. Mine."

"And I don't know why you insist on acting as though that's true when I have told you time and time again it's mine, too. I'm here. I'm injured. I've killed to protect you and Seth. It is *our* problem."

She closed her eyes briefly before sitting back down on the bed. "I know. I know. I just… We have to work together but that doesn't mean… You're hurt, Noah. We have to play to our strengths. You have to watch over Seth for me. You'll have to protect him and keep him safe. That's what I need from you. What *we* need from you."

"Addie," he all but seethed.

"I'm counting on you, so you have to do it."

"I'll be damned if I let that madman touch you. If I have to fight you *and* Grady to make sure that's the case."

"It's the only way. You're the only one who can keep Seth safe. I need you to do that for me, Noah. You're the only one I can trust with him."

"I can't let you do this, Addie."

"I know you must think I'm weak or stupid to have gotten mixed up in this thing—"

"I don't think that at all."

"Then you have to *trust* me." She took his hand in hers, Seth still happily slapping at his face while tears filled Addie's eyes. "Noah, I need you to protect him. He is the most important thing in the world to me. You're the only one who can do it. I know this kills you, but I wouldn't ask if it wasn't the only way. I can handle Peter as long as you can keep Seth safe."

He couldn't do this anymore. He was too tired. His head was pounding. Everything hurt, throbbed and ached. He couldn't fight her like this. He needed to build up his strength first. "We'll discuss it more tomorrow."

She sat there for a few seconds looking imperiously enraged before she let out a slow breath. "Fine." She seemed to really think over tomorrow. "We can talk more tomorrow. You need to rest."

"Yeah."

She started to move, but she still had her hand on his, so he grabbed it. Squeezed it. He needed her to understand that plans where she went off and put herself in danger just weren't an option. Not because she was weak. Not because of anything other than a selfish need to keep her close and safe.

Addie's and Seth's blue eyes peered at him, and he looked at them both, some brand-new pain in his chest. Not so much physical, this one.

"You're both important to me," he said resolutely. As much as he'd wanted to keep care and importance to himself, it was getting too dangerous to keep it bottled up. Too dangerous to try to keep her at arm's length. She had to know. "So important."

Some ghost of a smile flittered across her mouth before it was gone. Then she pressed her lips to his forehead, warm and smooth and somehow reassuring. "You're important to us," she whispered. "Now get some rest."

He wanted to fight it, but exhaustion won as Addie slipped out of the room, and Noah fell into a heavy sleep.

Chapter Twelve

Seth's schedule was so off it was nearly two in the morning before he was down for the night. Ty was asleep in the other bed in the cabin, having fixed up all the broken-in areas from earlier. Grady was asleep on the couch, snoring faintly.

Addie slipped into Noah's room and carefully laid Seth in his crib, watching him intently.

She would sacrifice anything for this boy. Including herself. It hadn't been an option before, but now she had people she could trust. People she could *entrust*.

Noah would protect him. The Carsons and Delaneys would give him love. Stability. Family.

She turned to Noah, asleep on the bed.

Knowing what she was going to do tomorrow she had to accept this might be the last time she spoke with him. She wouldn't allow herself to consider she might not survive, but she had to consider the fact that Noah might be so angry at her he'd never speak with her again.

She had to do what she had to do. For Seth, and for the only opportunity for a future that didn't involve running, losing or fighting for her life.

She slid onto the empty side of the bed, her heart beating a little too fast no matter that she was sure. Sure what she was going to do tonight, and sure what she was going to do tomorrow.

Noah stirred next to her and instead of staying on her own side, she scooted closer to him. The warmth of him, the strength of him. It was such an amazing thing that time and luck had brought her this man who wanted to protect her.

"Morning?" he murmured sleepily.

"No. Middle of the night." She should let him sleep. She should insist he rest. But she only had this one moment. She couldn't waste it. She pressed her mouth to his bearded cheek. "Would you do something for me?"

"In the middle of the night?"

"Well, it's a naked kind of something. Night seems appropriate."

She felt his whole body go rigid, and she was almost certain she could feel his gaze on her in the darkened room.

"Am I dreaming?" he asked suspiciously.

She allowed herself a quiet laugh and slid her hand under the covers and it drifted down his chest, his abdomen and then to the hard length of him. "Feels pretty real to me."

"That's a terrible line," he muttered, but he didn't shift away. Which might have been because of the injury on his opposite side, except he didn't shrink from her intimate touch. If anything he pushed into it.

"Noah, I want to be with you." She kissed his cheek, his jaw. "I've been pretending I don't, but it seems so silly to pretend with all of these horrible things going on. I don't want to pretend anymore, but if you don't want me—"

His mouth was on hers, fierce and powerful, before she could even finish the sentence. He carefully rolled onto his good side and his arms wound around her, drawing her tight against his body, trapping her own hand between them.

"I shouldn't," he said against her mouth.

"God knows I shouldn't." But he didn't let her go, and his mouth brushed her lips, her cheeks, her jaw.

"Why not?" she asked, if only because he hadn't stopped touching her, holding her, kissing her.

"You're too…" He trailed off.

When he never finished his sentence, she cupped his face, holding him there, a tiny inch away from her mouth. "I'm just me," she whispered before kissing him, something soft and sweet instead of intense and desperate.

That softness lingered, all those furtive glances they'd hidden over months of being under the same roof. All the hesitant touches immediately jerked away from. Longing glances behind each other's backs.

It had seemed so necessary then, and now it was stupid to have wasted all that time. Time they could have been together—getting to know each other, touching each other. And they hadn't only because she'd been certain he was too good and honorable to even look at her twice, and he'd been convinced she was too…*something*.

But they were just them, and for a little while they could be together. She tugged at his T-shirt, trying to pull it off him without hurting him. Carefully, she rid him of the fabric and discarded it on the other side of the bed.

His calloused hands slid under her shirt, the rough texture of his palms scraping against her sides and sending a bolt of anticipation through her. He lifted her shirt off her and dropped it.

"I closed the door, but Seth's asleep in his crib. We have to be quiet," she whispered.

He exhaled, something close to a laugh. "You think?" His breath fluttered across her cheek, his hands tracing every curve and dip of her body, cupping her breasts.

She groaned, trying to arch against him, bring him closer.

"Shh," he murmured into her ear, something like laughter in his voice.

Her heart squeezed painfully, because she wanted all of Noah's smiles and all of Noah's laughter and she was putting all of that in jeopardy. He was too noble, too sure to ever forgive her for going out on her own.

But that didn't change the fact that it needed to be done.

She trailed her hands across the firm muscles of his abdomen, sighing happily as she reached the waistband of his shorts. She moved to pull them down and off, give her full access to him, but he hissed out a breath and Addie winced, pulling away from him.

"I don't want to hurt you." No matter how much she wanted this, the thought of him in pain—

"I'll live. Keep touching me, I'll live."

She might have argued with him if his hands weren't on her. Tracing, stroking, pulling responses out of her body she didn't know were possible. She felt as though her skin were humming with vibrations, as though the room were filled with sparkling light instead of pitch-black.

They managed to remove the rest of each other's clothes without causing Noah any more pain—at least that he showed. Addie straddled his big, broad body, her heart beating in overtime, her core pulsing with need and something deeper in her soul knowing this was something meant. Elemental.

Noah was hers, and maybe she even loved him. She'd probably never get to explore that, but at least she got to explore this. Something she'd never felt, certainly not with this bone-deep certainty it was right. *They* were right.

She kissed him as he entered her, a long, slow slide of perfect belonging. His arms held her close and tight, and when he moved inside her, she sighed against his mouth and he sighed against hers.

He took her as though he was studying every exhale, every sigh, and making sure she did it again. And again, and again, with a kind of concentration and care no one had ever shown her. Until she was nothing but shaking pleasure, dying for that fall over into release.

"Noah."

"Addie."

It was the way he said her name, low and dark, full of awe, that propelled her over that sparkling edge of wonder. Noah pushed deep and held her tight and they lay there for who knew how long.

It didn't matter, because she wanted time to stop. Here. Right here.

But life didn't work that way. She slid off him, curling up into his good side. He murmured something, but she couldn't make it out.

"Sleep," she whispered, brushing a kiss below his ear.

"You, too," he murmured, holding her close.

She should. Sleep and rest, because tomorrow she would have to face a million hard things she'd been running from for too long.

So she gave herself this comfort. Noah's arms around her, his heart beating against hers. The fact that he'd been as desperate for her as she'd been for him, and out of something horrible that may change her life forever, at least she'd gotten this little slice of rightness.

It would give her strength, and it would give her purpose, and tomorrow she would find a way to end this all.

NOAH AWOKE TO the sound of a woman's voice. But it was all wrong. It wasn't Addie.

He opened his eyes, glancing at the woman sitting next to him on his bed.

"What the hell are you doing here?" he grumbled, his voice sleep-rusted and scathing against his dry throat. His body ached, just *ached*, and yet there was something underneath all that ache. A bone-deep satisfaction.

Except Addie wasn't here, and his cousin was.

"Good morning to you, too, sunshine," Vanessa offered cheerfully, bouncing Seth in her lap. "I don't know what the hell you do with these things, but he's a pretty cute kid."

"Where's Addie?"

"Can you hold him, or will that hurt your stitches?"

"Where the hell is Addie?"

Vanessa sighed gustily. "I know you've been shot and all, but there's no need to be so grumpy and demanding."

"Don't make me ask again, or you will regret ever stepping foot in this cabin."

Vanessa raised an eyebrow, and it was the kind of warning he should probably heed, but panic thrummed through his body, making it impossible to heed anyone's warning.

"You're hurt, so I'll give you a pass on that, Noah, but don't ever speak to me that way."

He struggled to get himself into a sitting position.

"Geez, you really are hurt." She wrinkled her nose. "Please tell me you're not naked under there."

He glared at her as Seth made a nosedive for him. With a wince, Noah caught the boy. Poor kid was too cooped up. He needed to crawl around and move, but the cabin wasn't the place for it.

And where the hell is Addie?

"I am not naked." At some point he'd pulled his boxers back on last night.

Vanessa clucked her tongue and shook her head. "First Grady. Now you."

"Now me what?"

"A Delaney, Noah. Really?"

"She's not a… Not…really. Where is she?"

"Well, she and Grady went somewhere."

"Where?" he growled.

"Sworn to secrecy, sorry."

The only thing that kept Noah's temper on a leash was the fact that if he started yelling at Vanessa, he'd likely scare Seth. And then Vanessa would make him pay for the yelling later. He took a deep breath, doing everything in his power to keep his anger from bubbling out of control.

"I know you don't like this, but you're hurt, and Addie had an idea and… Look, Grady promised he and Laurel would keep her safe. Ty's out seeing if he can get a truck up here to take you to the doctor. We're on baby patrol. It isn't so bad."

She'd done it anyway. After last night, after saying they'd talk about it, she'd gone and done some stupid, dangerous thing anyway. "She's going to put herself in harm's way. How is that not bad?"

"She's the one who brought this mob mess

to your doorstep, Noah. You'd be at your ranch, unharmed, if it weren't for her."

"She's not responsible for that. The man who's after her is."

"A man she had a kid with, Noah."

Slowly, because he couldn't believe Vanessa of all people would say that, he turned his head to face her. "You didn't just say that."

Vanessa shrugged, crossing her arms over her chest, adopting that pissed-off-at-the-world posture that seemed to propel her through life. "Well, it's true. You're paying because of the choices she made to get involved with someone awful. And yeah, the awful guy is at fault, but that…" She looked away, and Noah noticed a flicker of vulnerability he understood only because he'd once saved her from the abuses of his father.

"You're hurt," she said forcefully. "I get to be a little put out about my cousin being hurt."

He softened, only a fraction. "She's been hurt, too. You should be able to find some sympathy. You of all people."

Whatever vulnerability that had been evident in the cast of her mouth disappeared into hard-edged anger. "Then you need to understand that sometimes, not always but sometimes, people need to fight their own battles. Without you."

Which hit far too many insecurities of his own. He looked down at Seth, who was happily pulling at his chest hair. It might sting when he gave a strand a good tug, but it had nothing on knowing Addie was out there trying to fight her own battles.

She'd done that enough and he'd promised her no more, they were in this together, and she'd just ignored it. "I should have known what that was," he muttered.

"What *what* was?"

"Nothing. Never mind." But it had been a goodbye, plain and simple. And worse, so much worse, she'd chained him here under a responsibility he couldn't ignore. He scooted out of bed, hefting Seth onto his good side. "He needs to eat."

"No!" Seth tugged at his hair, making a sound Noah had a sneaking suspicion was his attempt at the word *hat*.

Noah strode out into the living room, Vanessa at his heels. Ty pushed in the door at the same moment, grim-faced and blank-eyed.

"We can't get out quite yet."

"How'd you stab me in the back and get Addie out of here?"

"They took the horses," Ty said with a shrug, clearly not worried about the back-stabbing.

Figured.

"Give me your hat," he demanded, holding out his hand to Ty.

Ty cocked his head, but handed the Stetson over after shaking some of the snow off it. Noah handed it to Seth, who squealed happily.

"If anything happens to her," Noah said, deadly calm, because he didn't have any other choice of what to be—he had to protect Seth—"God help all of you." With that he strode into the kitchen to get Seth some food.

Chapter Thirteen

Addie sat in the Carson ranch house for the third boring, alone day in a row and tried not to cry. None of this was going like it was supposed to.

The plan had been to install her at the Carson Ranch, making it look like she had Seth with her, and wait for the next ambush. They'd moved her, faked Seth's presence and acted as though they were trying to be sneaky while laying all sorts of clues that this is where they were.

But it had been three days. No matter how often she talked to Laurel on the phone about how sure Addie was that having Grady or one of the sheriff's deputies be a lookout was clearly keeping Peter away, Laurel insisted they keep going without Addie attempting to make personal contact with Peter.

Better to wait him out, Laurel insisted.

Let him feel like he was the one making the moves, not being lured.

Addie was learning that arguing with Laurel was absolutely pointless. The woman would do whatever she wanted, whatever she thought was best. Noah was like that. Grady, too. All the Carsons and all the Delaneys so sure they knew what was best and right.

Her included. She smiled a little at the thought. She was here because she'd been certain her being bait was the *only* way. She hadn't let Noah stop her.

But thinking about Noah only hurt. She missed him. She missed Seth like an open, aching wound. All there was to do in the silence of the Carson ranch house was miss them and worry about them and think about how mad Noah must be at her. If she managed to get over that she could only fret over the way it kept snowing and snowing and snowing.

She stared at her phone, trying to talk herself out of the inevitable panic call to Laurel. But she couldn't do it. This couldn't keep going. How long would she survive this endless, crazy-making waiting?

What awful things was Peter planning? He'd already proved he could wait as long as he pleased. He'd let her get settled here, hadn't he? Oh, she was now certain he was behind the poison and the fence-breaking. Little hints he was on the way, but enough doubt to cause her to wonder and worry, then talk herself out of it and settle in. Something like psychological warfare, and Peter was a pro.

She hit Call on Laurel's number in her phone, determined to talk Laurel out of the lookouts. She had to do this alone, without help or watchdogs. Maybe if she was persistent enough with Laurel—

"Addie, if you're calling me to tell me you can't do this—"

"I can't do this."

Laurel sighed. "Look, we've got some stuff brewing."

Addie straightened in her seat at the kitchen table. Noah and Seth missing like limbs she didn't know what to do without. "What does that mean?"

"Give me a sec."

Addie waited, trying not to think too hard about what *brewing* might mean.

"There. Some privacy. Listen, we've had five brand-new visitors to Bent in the past three days. That never happens. Now, none of them match the FBI's description of Peter, but that doesn't mean they don't work for him."

"I can't wait around for Peter if he's just going to send people. Maybe I should go to Bost—"

"You're not going anywhere." Laurel said it with the same kind of finality Noah had said it with days before. Addie hadn't listened to him. Why should she listen to Laurel?

"But Peter hasn't left Boston." If she went there. If she confronted him… She might die, sure, but maybe…

"According to the FBI, but who knows what they know."

"Laurel, they're the FBI. Maybe if I worked with them—"

"They clearly don't care enough. When I spoke with an agent all he could talk about was some other organized crime group they're infiltrating as part of the Monaghan case. They want a case. We want you safe. It's personal for us. Look, there was this guy at Grady's bar last night. He didn't match any of the descriptions we have on file as Peter's men, but maybe that's good. Maybe he sent someone new. He disappeared somewhere out of town last night, but if he comes back we'll be ready to tail him."

"What did he look like? Peter isn't big on hiring new men. His goons are all either friends from childhood or people his father used."

"Red-haired guy, about six foot maybe. Green eyes. Little scar next to his eye."

Addie's heart stopped, or at least it felt as though it did. "Laurel," she managed to whisper.

"You recognize him?"

"Laurel, that's Peter."

"What?"

"You just described Peter," Addie repeated, something like panic and relief swelling inside her chest. Thank God they could move forward. Peter was here.

And what would he do to her? She couldn't think about that. She had to think about the future. About ending this.

"No. The description we have of Peter is six-four, two forty, dark hair, blue eyes, with a tattoo on his wrist."

"No. No, that's not Peter. That's not Peter at all. He's shorter. Wiry. Red hair. Green eyes. The scar. I would know, Laurel. I would know."

Laurel swore. "So much for the damn FBI. Okay, I've got to radio this new description out to my men. Because he's here, Addie, and things are going to go down soon. Be smart. Be safe. Keep everything on you. Phone. Gun. Everything. Got it?"

Addie nodded before remembering she was on the phone. "Yeah, yeah, I got it." She didn't like carrying the gun around, so she'd started keeping a sheathed awful-looking knife in her pocket and the gun hidden in the kitchen. But she'd go get the gun. She'd be safe. She'd end this.

"I'll call again soon. Be safe." And with that the line went dead.

Addie took a deep breath. This was what she'd left Noah for. This was what she needed to do to keep Seth safe once and for all. She got to her feet, shaky with nerves, but filled with righteous determination.

Peter was here. Which meant he'd be *here* soon enough. They'd made it look like they were trying to keep her safe, but the locks were paltry and the windows weren't boarded. It'd be easy for anyone to sneak in.

When someone did, she'd have a deputy at her door, or Grady, or someone to save her and arrest Peter. If she could keep calm. If she could think clearly and make sure Peter made his intent known.

He would. She was sure he would.

"God, please, please, let that all be true," she whispered.

A loud smacking sound startled a scream out of her. She whirled at the sound of clapping, and her knees nearly buckled when Peter stepped around the corner, applauding as he smiled that horrible dead-eyed, evil-infused smile.

"Impressive performance, Addie."

She stood straighter, reminding herself to be strong. Reminding herself what she was doing. Saving Seth. Saving herself.

"Really, that was impressive," Peter said, gesturing at the phone clutched in her hand. "You should thank me for such a compliment."

"Go to hell."

Peter sighed heavily. "Always so rude. Your sister at least had some manners."

"Don't talk about her."

Peter rolled his eyes. "Well, this has gone on quite long enough, hasn't it? Though your fear and running has kept me quite entertained, and this darling little *family* you think you've created here. I can't decide if I want to kill them all and let you live with the guilt of *that* or something else entirely."

Addie smiled, some inner sense of calm and rightness stealing over her. Any second now, she'd be rescued and Peter would be put in jail. "Good luck, Peter," she offered faux-sweetly.

Any fake smiles or pretended enjoyment on his face died into flat, murderous fury. "I don't need your luck. I wonder if my son is old enough to remember watching me kill you."

Addie lifted her chin. "You'll never touch him."

There was a commotion somewhere in the back and Addie let out a shaky breath. They'd gotten his murder threat, which meant the deputy was coming to arrest Peter.

Except Peter's mouth twisted into a smile that sent ice down her spine. "Oh, you think that's your savior? You think your sad little plan was going to work on me? You're even dumber than your sister, Addie."

"She wasn't so dumb. She got Seth far away from you, didn't she?"

Peter lunged, grabbing her around the throat. She fought him off, and he didn't squeeze her hard enough to cut off her oxygen. He simply held her there, glaring at her with soulless green eyes no matter how she punched and kicked at him.

"It was fun while it lasted. Watching you run. Watching you settle in and convince yourself you were safe, bursting that bubble over and over again, but you stopped running. That really ruins my fun, Addie."

"Good," she choked out.

"Good indeed. I suppose it's time to find my son. I'm going to kill whoever has him in front of you. No one's going to save you, Addie, because right now in the back of this property a man who looks an awful lot like me is forcing a woman who looks quite a bit like you at gunpoint toward the mountains. And while your friends follow *him*, we'll be going in the opposite direction." He stuck his mouth right up against her ear. "No one's going to find you, Addie, and Seth will be all mine."

In a low, violent voice she cursed him. In the next second she felt a blinding pain, and the world went dark.

THE CONTINUOUS RAGE that had begun to exist like a tumor in Noah's gut never, ever let up in the three days of being stuck in the Carson cabin knowing Addie was somewhere out there without him to keep her safe. The only thing that kept him from exploding was the boy. Not just Noah's job to keep him safe, but watching Seth take hesitant steps from couch to wall and back again was…something. It eased a part of the horrible anger inside him, and he thanked God for it.

"No," the boy said, grinning happily up at him. Noah held out his hand and Seth slapped it with enthusiasm. Noah had taught a kid to high-five, and even amid the worry and anger, there was some joy in that. Some pride. Silly, maybe, but it was good. This was good.

This he would protect. "Gonna be a bruiser, aren't you, kid?" Noah murmured.

"Ma?"

Noah didn't let that rage show on his face. He kept his smile placid. "Mama will be home soon." Which was a promise he wasn't about to take lightly. Three days had healed his stitches well enough. He wasn't dizzy anymore, and he felt much stronger. Everything still hurt like hell, but it was bearable.

He was going to get out of here soon. Whether Ty and Vanessa wanted him to or not. He just had to formulate his plan and make sure Ty and Vanessa had the ability to protect Seth. So he could protect Addie.

Noah glanced over at Ty. Every morning and afternoon he went tracking out down the road in the vain hopes it was clear enough to get them all down the mountain.

They still had Vanessa's horse, but it couldn't carry them all, and Seth was too little to be traveling in this kind of weather, anyway.

Laurel checked in with Ty every evening, but no one would ever talk to Noah. The minute he grabbed the phone or tried to use his own, they hung up. Everyone refused to communicate with him, and it made the rage bigger, hotter. Rage was so much better than fear.

Every person in his life was a coward, and what was worse, he *felt* like one. No matter that watching Seth and protecting him was a noble pursuit. It felt like a failure not to be protecting Addie, too.

Vanessa was in the kitchen complaining about making dinner even though she was by far the best cook out of the three of them, and had insisted they stop trying as it all tasted like "poison."

Noah wasn't convinced his reheating a can of soup could poison someone, but Vanessa was happiest when she was complaining so he just let it go. Let her pound around and pretend she didn't like taking care of all three of them.

"No. Ha." Seth smashed Noah's hat onto his head. Noah tried to pay attention to their little game and not the fact that Ty's phone was trilling about two hours earlier than Laurel's usual check-in.

"Yeah?" Ty asked gruffly into his phone.

Seth continued to play his favorite game of taking the hat on and off, though he'd now added putting the hat on his own head to the mix.

"I see," Ty said, his voice devoid of any inflection.

Noah looked over at him, a heavy pit of dread in his stomach. He tried to reason it away, but it stuck like a weight, because Ty's expression was as blank as his voice.

In anyone else, Noah might have said he couldn't read that practiced blankness. Ty hadn't had it growing up, but he'd come home from the Army Rangers with the ability to completely blank all expression from his face.

It was just in this situation Noah knew the only reason he'd have to do that was if Addie'd been hurt.

"What happened?"

Ty didn't speak for a moment as he slowly placed his phone back in his pocket. But his gaze held Noah's. "The guy's in Bent."

The guy. Noah got to his feet, carefully maneuvering around Seth. "The guy's in Bent. Where's Addie?"

Ty stayed where he was. Still and blank. "It's all part of the plan."

Which did absolutely nothing with the way the dread was turning to fear, which he'd channel into fury. "Where is Addie?"

Ty blew out a breath. "If you can calm yourself, I'll explain it to you."

Calm? How was anyone *calm* knowing that a person he'd vowed to protect was just wandering around out there? A target. Aided by his family. He didn't know what was worse, that she'd made love to him and left to face evil alone, or that his family had helped her.

"They put Addie up at the ranch. Alone, but under the watch of either a deputy or Grady or even Laurel, depending on the time of day."

"Let me guess. It went so well. The bad guy's caught and Addie is one hundred percent safe."

Ty scowled. "The guy created a bit of a diversion. Instead of just trying to take Addie, he had another guy with him who made it look like *he'd* taken Addie. So, two guys with a woman apiece went in opposite directions. Since only one deputy was watching, he had to make his best guess on which one was actually Addie."

Noah laughed bitterly. Idiots. All of them. He strode for his rifle, which was hung up on the wall out of reach of Seth. He started gathering what he'd need. His coat, a saddlebag, a first aid kit.

"Noah, you can't just leave," Vanessa said.

"Like hell I can't."

"What about Seth?" Vanessa demanded.

"You'll keep him safe."

"Addie asked *you* to do that."

"And I asked you all to keep Addie safe. She's not. She's with a mobster who's been chasing her for a year, who will very likely kill her once he finds out where Seth is. Who in this damn town is a better tracker than I am?" he demanded, glancing back and forth from Ty to Vanessa and back again.

"I'm not half-bad," Ty said. "Army Ranger and all. Besides, the deputy is tracking one of them. It could be Addie."

"And it could not be. Regardless, a mobster and his buddy have two women. Both are likely going to end up dead if someone doesn't do something."

"Let me do it," Ty said. "I can track as well as you. And I don't have a gunshot wound."

"You can't track as well as I can *here. I'm* the one who knows Bent and those mountains better than anyone. *I* helped track Laurel down when she was kidnapped. No one, and I mean *no one*, is better equipped to do this thing than I am. Not Laurel's idiot deputies, and not you or Grady. So I am taking that horse. You are arming yourself to the teeth. You die before you let anyone harm that child. And I will die before I let anyone harm Addie."

"You're hurt, Noah."

"I'll damn well live." Because he didn't think he could if something happened to Addie. So he couldn't let that happen.

Chapter Fourteen

Addie woke up groggy, her head pounding. It felt like a hangover, but in painful detail she remembered all too well what it was.

Peter had hit her with something and knocked her out. Nausea rolled in her gut, and she wished she knew more about head trauma or concussions. Was she seriously hurt? Was she going to die?

You will not die. Not until Seth is safe. Seth. Noah. She had to hold on to the belief that she could end this for them.

She took a deep breath in and slowly let it out. She took stock of her body as she looked around her surroundings.

She was cold. So cold. She smelled hay and horse. The walls were slats of wood and… She was in the stable. In one of the horses' individual pens. Tied to the wooden slats and sitting in the hay. Cold without a coat on in the middle of winter, head throbbing from who knew what kind of head trauma.

But she was not far from the Carson Ranch. At least, she didn't think. This didn't look exactly like the stables close to the house. Everything out here was a little dilapidated, and the hay certainly wasn't new. It was gray and icy. She knew for a fact someone had been doing Noah's chores around the ranch to keep the horses and cows alive.

So maybe she wasn't at the Carson Ranch at all.

She couldn't panic. Even as it beat in her chest like its own being, she couldn't let it win. She had to be smart. She had to *think*.

She was tied to the wooden slats of the stables with a rope. The wooden slats didn't look particularly sturdy, but the rope on her wrists was tight and rough.

She gave her arms a yank and the wooden slat moved. She paused and listened, but there were no sounds except the howling wind. Was Peter around?

She gave her arms another yank. Again the wooden slat moved, even creaked a little as though she'd managed to splinter it. She tried not to let the hope of it all fill her with too much glee. She had to focus. Listen for Peter. Be smart. She had to be smart.

Still there was nothing but silence. No footsteps. None of Peter's nasty comments. She didn't feel the oppressive fear of his presence. So she kept yanking. Harder and harder with fewer pauses between times. Each time Peter didn't appear, she felt emboldened to move faster.

She lost track of how many yanks, of the burning in her wrists from the way the rope rubbed, because all she could think about was escape. She could outrun Peter in the snow. While he fancied himself a hunter and an outdoorsman, she knew from her sister he did it in upscale lodges with guides doing most of the work.

She'd been living in Wyoming for months now, doing somewhat physical labor by keeping house. She wasn't soft like Peter. She could outrun him. She knew at least some of the area. She could win.

She had to believe she could win.

She gave another hard yank and it was followed by the sound of wood splintering. Her momentum sent her forward, and since she didn't have the arms to reach out and catch herself as her wrists were tied together, she maneuvered to her side and fell that way.

She blew out a breath, not moving for a few seconds as she lay on the icy hay. Peter still didn't come running.

She laughed out a breath. She'd done it. She'd actually done it. But she had to focus and be careful and smart. Peter could be anywhere, and with her hands tied behind her back and a piece of wood dangling from the rope, she couldn't fight him off. Her only option right now was to escape.

And go where?

It was winter in Wyoming and she had no coat. She had some kind of head injury and her hands were tied behind her back.

Taking her chances with the elements was a much better option than taking her chances with Peter. Someone would find her. They knew she'd been taken, diversion or not. Someone would find her. She had to believe that.

She got to her feet, leaning against the wall as dizziness washed over her. She was definitely not 100 percent, but she could do this. Her legs were fine.

Once the dizziness settled, she took a step away from the wall. She wasn't completely steady on her feet, but it would have to do. Maybe Peter had tied her up and left her to die from exposure, but she had a bad feeling he wasn't done with her yet.

If she escaped now she could press charges. She could tell the FBI everything she knew and they'd have to arrest him for all the other things as well. She'd never had any evidence he'd killed Kelly, but she had proof that he'd tried to kill *her* in the here and now.

It had to be enough.

Carefully, she poked her head out of the stall she'd been in. The entire stable was empty. Ramshackle. She had no idea where she was. She'd never seen this building before. All of the buildings she'd seen on Carson property were certainly old and a little saggy, but cared for. No holes in the sides or roofs caving in like this building had.

So, not on Carson property, but people were looking for her. So all she had to do was run.

And hope she didn't end up in the mountains. Alone. Overnight.

There was a giant door on one side of the stable, but she wasn't stupid enough to go out that way. If Peter was still around, he'd see that. So she needed a window or a loose board or something. It was still dangerous, but she'd cut down as much chance of detection as she could.

She searched the stable and found two long-ago-broken windows. There wasn't an easy way to leverage herself up and out with the jagged edges of glass, the height, or her hands tied behind her back. So she went to the holes in the walls, poking and prodding at the wood around them as best she could without the full use of her arms.

It wasn't easy going and frustration was threatening, but she couldn't let it overwhelm her. Couldn't let—

She frowned as the faint smell of gasoline started to filter through the air. She hadn't seen any machinery in the stables that might be leaking old fuel. Panic tickled the back of her throat, but she swallowed it away. Maybe it was a side effect of the head injury.

Except then she heard laughter and everything inside of her roiled with futility as Peter's face appeared in the hole she'd been working on.

"Here's Johnny!" he offered all too happily before kicking at the loose boards around the hole—creating an even bigger one. The debris flew at her and she tried to move back so it wouldn't hit her, but she lost her balance and fell back on her butt, unable to stop from falling all the way onto her back since she couldn't use her hands to hold her up.

Peter stepped through the large hole he'd kicked and loomed over her. "Did you think you'd escape?" Peter laughed as if this was all just fun for him, to torture someone. To hurt someone. What had been warped in him to feel good at another's misfortune?

The smell of gasoline got even stronger, and Addie tried not to let fear destroy all the courage she had inside her.

But Peter calmly pulled a lighter out of his pocket, flicking the small flame to life in the frigid air between them, and the smell of gas was only making her feel even more dizzy than she already had.

"Actions have consequences, Addie. Your sister learned that. The hard way. I thought you might have more sense, but I see I was wrong. You stopped running. You tried to fight. No one fights me and wins."

"I've been doing an okay job. You don't have Seth."

"But I will. The question is whether I let you die here, or in front of him."

The smell of gas was making her sick to

her stomach. The flick of the lighter. He was going to kill her.

She breathed through that fear, because he would want to save himself. He'd want to be far enough away before he set this place on fire. It would give her a chance. It had to give her a chance.

"If you tell me where he is, I might just let you out. Let you run again. If not..." He shrugged and flicked the lighter again.

"You'll never find him. Ever."

"I guess you're dead, then." And he dropped the lighter.

HORSEBACK TOOK TOO damn long. Especially with the snow and the isolation of the cabin. Carson Ranch was too far away. Everything was stacked against Noah, including the pain ricocheting through his side where he might have already busted his stitches.

He wouldn't let any of that stop him.

Besides, if he'd been in a vehicle he would have to go down through Bent. On horseback—slower or not—he could cut up through the valleys where there weren't any roads and enter the property through the northeast pastures. It'd be more of a surprise approach, and maybe he'd even catch Peter with Addie trying to get out.

The closer he got to Carson property, the less he let his brain move in circles. He was focused. He was determined. For Seth and for Addie, he'd do whatever it took.

"Stop!"

The order seemed to have come out of nowhere, and Noah would have ignored it if not for the glint of a gun from behind the tree line next to him. He brought his horse to a stop, surreptitiously eyeing his surroundings, what options he had.

"Carson?"

Noah stared at the glint of gun. He couldn't see the person and he didn't recognize the voice, but whoever it was continued on.

"Get behind the trees. Now."

He followed the harsh order if only because if it was someone out to hurt him, they would have done it by now. He nudged his horse back into the trees and eyed the man.

Crouched behind a rock was one of the Bent County deputies. He looked more like a boy to Noah, but Noah dismounted and looped the reins of the horse to the closest tree. He crouched next to the *kid*, ignoring the throbbing pain in his side.

"I've got one of the fugitives in my sights," the deputy offered. He held out a hand. "Deputy Mosely. Laurel made sure we knew what all the Carsons looked like so we didn't actually hurt the wrong person." He frowned. "She didn't tell me you'd be coming as backup, though."

Noah shook the man's hand and said nothing. He was more interested in scanning the valley below the rocks. There were two lone figures standing next to a ramshackle building that had been an outhouse long before Noah's lifetime.

He couldn't make out faces or even heights, but his stomach sank. "That's not Addie," Noah said flatly. Even from this distance he knew that wasn't the shade of her hair. It was too white blond, not honeyed enough.

"What? How… You don't know that." The man shifted in his crouch and brought a pair of binoculars to his eyes.

"I know that," Noah replied, striding back to his horse. He didn't even need to take a look through the binoculars. "Which way did the other couple go?"

"I don't… The opposite. You can't just…" The kid straightened his shoulders, adopting what Noah supposed was meant to be an intimidating look. "Mr. Carson, I would kindly suggest you don't try to get in the way of the Bent County Sheriff's Department's actions."

Noah snorted and didn't stop moving. "The Bent County Sheriff's Department can go to hell."

Deputy Mosely sputtered. Hell, was this kid just out of the academy or something?

"What are you going to do?" Noah demanded, gesturing toward the couple in the valley.

"Not that it's your business, but I'm going to radio Deputy Delaney and follow her orders to—"

Noah rolled his eyes. No damn way was he letting this go even more wrong. He lifted his rifle and pointed it toward the couple below.

"Sir, put the weapon down immediately…"

Noah looked through the sight, saw his target—the man's arm, because he wasn't an idiot or scared of doing the wrong thing while in uniform—and shot, ignoring the fact that the deputy had pulled his gun. The kid wasn't going to shoot a fly, let alone Noah himself.

"You…" The man gaped at him, like a damn grounded fish.

"Well, go arrest him," Noah ordered, putting his gun back in its soft case. "Get her back wherever she came from. Send everyone you've got available in the *opposite direction of…*" He trailed off as he noticed something not quite right in the horizon. Weirdly hazy.

He whirled around and there was a billow of smoke off to the west. "There," he said, already moving for Vanessa's horse. "Send everyone there. North point of Carson property. Follow the smoke."

"You can't just—" the deputy called after him.

Noah urged his horse into a run. "I just did." Vanessa's horse sped through the snow, agile and perfect, and Noah thanked God they had the kind of animals who could handle this.

Now he just had to make it across the entire north pasture to whatever was on fire and hope he could get there quick enough to save Addie, because he had no doubt she was somewhere in the middle of it.

God help the man who hurt her.

Chapter Fifteen

It turned out Addie had learned something in school. Stay low during a fire. Cover your mouth. Use your hands to feel out a possible escape route.

It was difficult to nudge her shirt over her nose with only the use of her chin and neck, but she managed after a while. Crawling was even more difficult with her hands tied behind her back, but she forced herself through an awkward, careful crab walk.

It didn't matter, though. There was no escape. There was only smoke and heat. Everything around her was burning. *Burning.*

She held on to the insane hope Peter had set himself on fire in the blaze instead of only trapping her inside. Even as the roaring of the fire creaked and crackled. Even as she had no idea where she was in the stables, let alone if she was close to some escape.

But she kept moving. Kept blinking against the sting of the smoke, kept thinking past the horrible sounds around her. She could lie down and die, but where would that leave Seth?

And Noah? What would happen to Noah?

She had to keep fighting.

So she scooted around, even as it got harder and harder to breathe. Even as she was almost convinced she was crawling in endless circles she'd never escape. But anything was better than stopping, because stopping would be *certain* death instead of just maybe death.

She thought she heard her name, and she was more than sure it was in her head, but she moved toward it anyway. It was either death or some guardian angel.

"Addie."

Some unknown voice above the din of the fire, and still she crawled toward it. She paused in her crawling. She tried to call back, but nothing came out of her scorchingly painful throat except a rusty groan muffled by her shirt.

Useless. She resumed crawling. Toward that faint sound.

"Addie."

"Noah." It came out scratchy and sounding

nothing like his name and really she had to be hallucinating, because how would *Noah* be here? He was watching Seth.

Oh, God, he had to be watching Seth. She crawled faster, ignoring the way she couldn't see, the way her whole body felt as if it were swaying. She moved toward Noah's voice. Whether it was a hallucination or not, it had to be her escape.

She tried to keep her breathing even, but it was so hard. Tears stung her eyes, a mix of emotion and stinging from the flames around her. It was a searing, nauseating heat and she kept crawling toward it. Toward salvation.

Or is it your death?

Out of nowhere, arms were grabbing her, and there was somehow something cool in all the ravaging heat. Then it was too bright, and she had to squeeze her eyes shut against all that light.

For a moment she lay there in the foreign icy cold, eyes squeezed shut, almost certain she'd died.

But hands were pulling her to her feet, and then to take steps, and she let whoever it was lead her. Wherever they were going, it was away from that horrible fire.

"Just a ways farther."

She opened her eyes even though they burned like all the rest. "Noah." She could hear the fire raging behind them, even as he pulled her forward in the drifts of snow.

"Come on, sweetheart, a little ways farther."

"Am I dreaming?"

He glanced back at her, but continued to pull her forward. "Feels pretty unfortunately real to me," he said. There was no hint of a smile, and yet she wanted to laugh. Those were her words.

This was real. The misty gray twilight that hurt her eyes after the dark smoke of the stable. Noah, *Noah*, leading her to safety.

"Where's Seth?" Her voice sounded foreign to her own ears, scraped raw and awful, but she only barely felt the seething pain beyond the numbness. Still, the words were audible somehow.

"He's safe. That I promise you. Where's Peter?"

"I don't…" They reached the tree line and finally Noah allowed her to stop walking, but she was pulled into the hard press of his chest. He swore ripely, over and over again even as his hands methodically moved over her body.

"I don't think we have time for sex," she said, attempting a joke.

"I'm checking you for injuries," he replied, clearly not amused.

Her arms fell to her sides as Noah cut the rope holding her hands together.

"No broken bones," he muttered. "I imagine you have some kind of smoke inhalation." He pulled her back, studying her face intently. "What hurts?"

"I don't..." She couldn't think. All she could see was the blazing fury in his gaze. "How are you here?"

"I wasn't going to let him take you, and apparently I'm the only one in this whole world with any sense. You running off. Laurel having *children* watch you who follow the wrong damn people." His hands gripped her arms, his eyes boring into her. "I swear to God if you ever do anything like this again, I'll lock you up myself."

He was so furious, so violently angry, and yet his grip was gentle, and he kept all that violence deep within him. This man who'd been shot trying to keep her safe, and was now pulling her out of burning buildings.

"Noah..." She didn't know what to say, so she leaned into him and pressed her mouth to his. Everything hurt except that.

His hand smoothed over her hair and he

kissed her back, the gentleness in the kiss the complete antithesis of everything she could tell he was feeling.

She'd believed she could take Peter on alone—well, with the help of Laurel and Grady and the deputies, but mostly on her own. And she knew, even now with a bullet hole in his side to tell him otherwise, Noah thought he could take Peter down bare-handed.

But in this moment, and in his kiss, Addie realized something very important. They could only survive this *together*.

"You don't have a coat," he murmured, immediately shrugging out of his and putting it around her. She didn't even know how her body reacted to it. She felt numb all over, but somehow she was standing.

"You'll be cold now."

"I have more layers on," he returned, scanning the horizon around him. "Where'd he go?"

"I don't know." She pulled away and looked back at the burning stable, feeling an unaccountable stab of grief even with her renewed sense of purpose. "I was hoping he'd burned himself up."

Noah squinted down at the building. "Not

likely. There." He pointed at something. Addie squinted, too, but she saw nothing.

"Tracks," Noah said flatly. "Coming and going."

"How can you see that? It's been snowing and—"

"I can see it." His gaze returned to her. "You need a doctor."

"Over my dead body are we separating ever again, Noah Carson. It's you and me against Peter, or you're going back to Seth right this instant."

He opened his mouth and she could tell, just *tell*, he was going to argue, so she gave his chest a little push until he released her. "We don't have time to argue, and if you can't see that the only way we survive this, the only way we *win* this, is together, I don't have time to convince you."

"You're right we don't have time to argue," he muttered, taking her hand. "But you better keep up until we get to Annabelle."

"Who's Annabelle?"

"Our ride."

NOAH WASN'T SERIOUSLY worried about Peter being on the run.

At first.

After all, Addie was safe with Noah, and Ty and Vanessa together could take care of any lone psychopath who clearly wasn't as good of a criminal as he fancied himself. So far Peter'd had ample opportunity to really hurt Addie and he hadn't done it. He kept giving her opportunities to escape. Maybe he expected her to die in the fire, but he certainly hadn't made sure.

Maybe he didn't want to hurt Addie. Maybe he just wanted his son back. Noah would never let that happen, but it soothed him some to think maybe this could all be settled without Addie getting hurt.

He glanced back at where she sat behind him on Annabelle's back. Her face was sooty and her breathing sounded awful. She was clearly struggling, and still she watched the ground and the trail of Peter's footprints they were following on horseback.

Any magnanimous thoughts he'd had toward Peter Monaghan obliterated to ash. He had left Addie to die in that fire. A painful, horrible death. No, he was no kindhearted criminal who couldn't bring himself to end her life on purpose. He wanted her tortured. He was evil.

He needed to be stopped. Ended. So Seth

never had to grow up and truly know what it was like to have that kind of soullessness in a father.

Noah would make sure of it.

He led Annabelle next to Peter's footprints, shaking his head at how easy this all was. Scoffing at the FBI and everyone else who hadn't caught this moron.

Until he realized that the footprints doubled back and followed Noah's original ones. Back to where he'd stopped with Deputy Mosely. Then carefully going along the trail of his horse's prints.

It had snowed, but lightly. There'd been no major wind. Since the snow had been a crusty, hard ice, the horse's stuck out.

With a sinking nausea, Noah realized Peter was going to use Noah's own damn trail to lead Peter to Seth.

"How did Peter get a horse?" Addie wondered aloud, her voice still low and scratchy.

Noah tensed and tried to think of a way to explain it that wouldn't lead her to the conclusion he'd drawn. Not that Peter had gotten a horse, but that he was following Noah's horse's tracks. Noah tried to think of how to hurry without drawing attention to the fact that they needed to hurry.

Vanessa and Ty could handle Peter, but Noah was slowly realizing Peter had more in his arsenal than Noah had given him credit for.

"Noah," she rasped in his ear. "Tell me what you're thinking."

He swore as the footprints stopped and suddenly vehicle tracks snaked out across the snow. Peter clearly wasn't alone anymore. He had what Noah assumed was some kind of snowmobile, and at least one man helping him.

A vehicle that could traverse the snow better and faster than his horse. Following his tracks back to the cabin. The only hindrance would be trees, but that wouldn't make the tracks unfollowable on foot.

"Noah... Noah, please tell me this isn't what I think it is," Addie said, her voice shaky from cold or nerves, he didn't know.

He couldn't tell her, so he kicked Annabelle into a run. He didn't want to push the horse this hard, but they had to get to Seth. "What do you think it is?" he asked through gritted teeth as wind rushed over them, icy and fierce. If he was cold without his jacket, fear and determination kept him from feeling it.

Addie didn't answer him. She held on to

him, though, the warmth of her chest pressing into his back. She was careful to hold him above his wound, but sometimes her arm slipped and hit him right where it already ached and throbbed.

But the pain didn't matter. What Addie thought didn't matter. All that mattered was getting to Seth before Peter did.

Addie held on tight as they rode hard toward the Carson cabin. Much like his desperate ride in the opposite direction, the land seemed to stretch out in never-ending white, and there was no promise in the beautiful mountains of his home. There was only danger and failure.

Still, Noah urged Annabelle on, and the horse, bless her, seemed to understand the hurry. As they got closer to the cabin, Noah eased Annabelle into a slower trot. The snowmobile tracks veered one way, but if Noah went the opposite they could sneak up on the back of the cabin through the wooded area.

"Why are we slowing down? He's got so much time on us if he was in a vehicle. We can't let him get to Seth."

"Vanessa and Ty will fight him off."

"He isn't alone," Addie said flatly. "Someone had to bring him that snowmobile."

Noah ducked and instructed her to do so as well as they began to weave their way through the trees, bobbing around snow-heavy limbs. He didn't need the snowmobile's tracks anymore. "They couldn't cut through the trees with the vehicle. It looks like someone walked this way and instructed them how to get around this heavily wooded part. So they didn't approach the cabin this way as a group. That's good."

"Is it?"

"Ideally, it gives us the element of surprise, but that can't be all. We need to slow down, think and plan. We need to end this."

She laughed bitterly. "I keep thinking that and we keep running this way and that."

"You said we needed to work together. Well, here we go. Peter must think you're dead. He has to." Which got Noah thinking… "Addie, if he thinks you and Seth are dead…"

"How could we possibly do that? What would it solve? We'd always be in danger if he found out."

"Not if he's in jail, which is the least of where he belongs. Convincing him you're dead would just be insurance. A layer of safety on top of all the other layers."

"I… I guess, but do we have time to figure out how to do that? We have to make sure Seth is safe."

"All you have to do is make sure Peter doesn't see you."

"I don't give a… We just need to get Seth. That's all I care about."

Noah understood that, whether he wanted to or not. But he couldn't let fear or panic drive him. That's what had led him to the Carson Ranch, and yes, he'd saved Addie in the process, but he'd also led Peter straight to Seth.

"You're going too slow," Addie insisted, desperation tingeing her voice.

"I can't imagine what it must be like, the fear and the panic, but we can't let it win. You know I wouldn't let anything…" He trailed off, because he *had* let things happen to her and Seth. "We have to end this, which means we have to be smart. Leading with emotion, with fear, with letting someone else call the shots, is what got us here, Addie. If we'd fought straight off, if you'd stayed in the cabin, if I hadn't flown after you half-cocked… We're mucking things up right and left, and we can't keep doing it. Because Seth *is* at stake."

He felt as much as heard Addie's sharp

intake of breath, feeling bad for speaking so harshly to her, but it was all true. They couldn't keep *reacting*, they had to plant their feet and act.

"Maybe you're right," she said softly into his ear as he brought Annabelle to a stop. They were deep in the woods, but he knew exactly where the cabin was though he couldn't see it though the snow and thick trees. About a hundred yards straight ahead.

"So, let's figure out a plan. A real plan. A *final* plan. One that brings you both home safe."

"Home?" she echoed.

"Bent is your home, Addie. Yours and Seth's. From here on out, it'll always be your home." He'd fight a million battles and risk life and limb to make it so.

Chapter Sixteen

Addie let Noah help her off the horse. The horse was panting heavily, and Addie couldn't help but breathe in time with her. Too shallow. Too fast.

But Noah was right. No matter that she wanted to tear through the woods screaming, shooting at anyone who got in her way with Noah's rifle, until Seth was safely in her arms. It wouldn't do the thing that needed to be done.

Seth. She needed Seth's *permanent* safety at the top of her list. Not just these snatches of time with it-didn't-matter-how-many people protecting him. She needed to give him safety, stability, a *home*.

Bent is your home. She hadn't realized how desperately she wanted that to be true until Noah had said it, had held her gaze steady and sure. Underneath all that surety, she'd seen…she was sure she'd seen the kind of bone-numbing fear and fury she felt in her soul at Seth being in direct line of danger.

"If we're going to convince him Seth's dead, we have to get Seth away first."

Noah nodded, his jaw set. She could see the way he thought the problem through. She could see the same thing she felt.

How? How? How?

"I'm not usually the one with the plan. I'm the one who acts," he muttered.

"Well, the other plans haven't worked. Maybe you need to be."

He flicked a glance at her, eyebrows drawing together. "We don't know how many men he has."

"There were only tracks to one vehicle, right? So it can't be more than a couple. Maybe four of them altogether. And there's four of us. It's a fair fight."

"Really," Noah replied drily.

"It's close, anyway."

"We'll go with four men," Noah said, staring through the trees. "Armed, probably better than us." Noah glanced at her again. "Do you think he meant to kill you?"

"I don't think he cares either way. He wants

me hurt and scared, but what he really wants is Seth."

"You don't think he has some kind of feeling for the mother of his child?"

Addie had to look away. She should tell him. Explain the whole thing. Except they didn't have time for that right now. "It's complicated."

Noah rubbed a hand over his beard. "There's a secret passageway into the cabin. The guy who shot me saw me come out of it, but surely he couldn't relay that information back to Peter considering you killed him."

Killed him. She'd killed a man. And she was prepared to kill another. If the opportunity arose, she needed to be willing to kill Peter. Seth's father.

She steeled herself against that soft spot. Yes, Peter was Seth's father, and maybe Seth would never fully understand the threat his father posed. She prayed he didn't. That he'd never fully understand. Even if it meant he grew to hate her.

Seth was the most important thing. His life. His future. His happiness.

"So, we'll create a diversion," Noah said, steel threaded through his voice. He might not be used to being the one making the plans, but he was certainly used to being in charge. "I'll be careful and try to sneak in the cabin, but the most important thing is getting you into the secret passage. If I can get to Ty and Vanessa, we can work out how to get Seth to you through the passage. If we can, we'll get Vanessa, too, and you two can figure out how to make it look like something happened to Seth while Ty and I fight them off."

"That leaves you vulnerable. Four against two."

"We don't know they have four, and I'd bet on me and Ty anyhow."

"You said yourself they probably have better weapons."

"You can't beat the bad guy without taking some risks, Addie. I think we can both agree Seth is the most important thing, right? It's why you left. It's why you let yourself be bait. I lost sight of that, took Seth's safety for granted in the face of a danger to yours, and look where it led. Right here. It's my fault Peter figured out how to get to Seth, because I lost sight of that one thing. Well, not again. I'd die before I let anything happen to him."

Addie blinked back the tears that stung her eyes. She'd come to that same conclusion, too, and as much as the idea of losing Noah physically hurt, Seth… Seth was the priority.

"All right," Addie managed, though her voice was scratchy from the fire, from the cold, from emotion. "We'll go up to the cabin, scope it out. You'll show me the secret passageway. We'll get me in, then I'll wait."

"I'll see if I can get to Ty or Vanessa without detection. You stay in that secret passageway until we get you Seth, or we can get Vanessa and Seth in. We'll keep the rest occupied."

"What if—"

"That's the plan. We focus on the plan. If we get there and we can't get to the secret passageway, we'll come back here and reevaluate. Now we move. We have to be silent. They can't know we're there yet, but most especially they can't catch sight of you."

"Most important after Seth, that is."

Noah nodded. "We'll promise each other, here and now, everything we do is to protect that boy." He held out his gloved hand.

Dwarfed and warmed by his coat, she slid her hand out of the sleeve and shook Noah's. "Agreed."

Noah turned to the horse, pulled some things out of the bags that hung off the saddle. Feed and water. A blanket. He took those few minutes to make the horse comfortable. "If you and Vanessa get out, you need to be able to make your way back to Annabelle. We're going to cover our tracks, so you have to be able to get back here blind."

Addie swallowed. She didn't know the area at all, especially out here. "How?"

Noah considered the question, then pulled a small Swiss Army knife out of his pocket. "We'll mark the trees." He gave her a once-over. "I don't have a gun to give you, so you'll have to take this once we're done. You need some kind of protection."

Protection. She pulled out the knife she'd managed to stick into the back of her pants back at the ranch. It hadn't helped her against Peter because she'd been trying to lure him, not hurt him, and then he'd knocked her out.

She wouldn't be so stupid next time.

"I have this."

Noah raised his eyebrows, since it was a pretty impressive knife she'd found with a bunch of hunting supplies in one of the supply closets at the ranch. It had been the easiest-to-conceal weapon she'd been able to find that had a kind of sheath that would keep her safe from the blade.

"That'll do. Let's get started." With that, Noah began a path toward the cabin, carefully marking a network of trees with little *x*'s a person would have to know were there to find, while Addie carefully covered their tracks in the snow.

When they could start to see the cabin through the trees, their pace slowed, but they didn't stop. As silently as they could, they crept forward, still working, always watching.

Addie could make out the snowmobile, empty and parked to the side of the cabin. But as her gaze searched the space around the cabin, the woods around her, she saw no sign of any men. Only their footprints around the snowmobile.

Noah nodded toward the cabin and she followed him, wordlessly stepping into the bigger prints he left. They didn't have time to cover these. Not yet.

With one last look around the yard and tree line, Noah stuck his fingers into some crevice Addie hadn't even seen and seemingly magically pulled, amassing snow in a large hill behind it, until a very small door opened.

He gestured her forward, and even though it was dark and who knew what all lay inside, Addie knew she had to crawl in there. So on a deep breath, she did. Squeezing through the opening and contorting her body into the dark space that was some hidden part of the cabin. She re-sheathed her knife and shoved it where it had been down the back of her pants.

"Stay inside," Noah said, worry reflecting in his dark eyes even if it didn't tremble in his voice. "On the opposite side is another door, but it's covered by the fridge. If we can get Seth, or Vanessa and Seth, to you, it'll be through there. There's a peephole here." He pointed to a hole in the wall that allowed her to see out into the backyard. "But there's no way to see inside."

"Okay." She tried to keep her mind on those instructions. On the plan they'd created together.

"Stay put until one of us gets you. Promise?"

She didn't want to promise that. There were so many what-ifs in her mind.

"The only exception to that promise is if you know Seth is in immediate danger. Okay? Deal?"

She still didn't love that deal, because she wanted to protect him, too, but... Well, they'd seen how well that worked out when Noah had rushed to protect her. She was glad to be alive, and Peter probably would have found Seth eventually, anyway, but...

But Seth had to come first. "Deal."

Noah nodded and started to push the door closed, then he swore roughly. Addie jumped, thinking they'd been caught, but he only reached forward and pulled her to him.

"Do you want your coa—"

Then his mouth was on hers, rough and fierce. A kiss of desperation, anger and, strangely, hope.

"I love you, Addie," he murmured against her mouth.

And before she could even think of what to say to *that*, Noah pushed the door closed with an audible *click*.

She was in the dark and alone, and she had to sit with *that* and wait.

I love you.

What kind of man said I love you before he closed you into a secret passageway while mobsters were after you and the baby in your care?

But neither anger nor bafflement took hold quite like she intellectually thought they would. Instead, she felt only the warm glow of *love*. Love. Noah—taciturn, grumpy, sweet, good Noah—had said he *loved* her.

After she'd spent so much of the time before Peter had come being afraid to even think he might look at her with more than blind disinterest, Noah *loved* her.

She couldn't possibly predict what would happen with all this, if they'd all survive unscathed or not, but Noah loved her, and Seth needed her.

For Seth, she could endure anything. With love, she could face any challenge.

NOAH MADE QUICK work of covering up the snow around the door and his tracks to and from the secret passageway. He searched his surroundings, listening for any faint hint at where everyone was. It left a terrible feeling in his gut. Everything was too quiet.

He moved soundlessly through the trees to make a circle around the cabin, checking the perimeter. Once he was satisfied there was no lookout on this side, he focused on the tracks around the cabin.

There were quite a few sets of footprints, though he could assume the shallow ones were old and filled with new snow. The heavy ones… He counted, tried to make out different footwear, tried to decide who was who based on where they'd come from.

Three men, it looked like, though looks could be deceiving. There was the pair of tracks that had followed Noah's original ones. They came out of the woods, then went down the road. Then the vehicle tracks.

Only one set of footprints went toward the cabin. The other two fanned out down the road.

So they had two men watching the road for intruders, and one man—probably Peter, though he couldn't be sure—on the inside.

His odds were good, because if he only had men looking out from the road, the Carsons could kill Peter before he could make a peep.

But Noah wouldn't be that cocky this time around. He'd still be careful. Cautious. He glanced at the snowmobile. No one was getting away on that thing. He didn't want Addie to be seen, and Seth wouldn't be safe on it. So it was useless to him.

He needed to make it useless to them as well. Moving as quickly but as quietly as he could, he lifted the panel to the engine and then used his Swiss Army knife to snap any wires or tubes he could find. He paused, waiting for someone to fly out of the trees or a bullet to come whizzing by, but nothing happened.

He crept closer to the cabin. The windows were boarded up, so there was no way to see in. He frowned at the door, because it appeared to be cracked open.

Noah moved toward it, gaze still darting behind him and at the road. The closer he got, the more he realized he could hear someone talking in there.

"You lot seem to think you're awfully tough."

Noah reached for the rifle on his back. Still, no matter how he maneuvered himself, he couldn't see inside the crack of the door. He could only hear.

He was tempted to bust in and start shooting, but he couldn't do it without knowing what was on the other side. He couldn't risk his brother or his cousin any more than he could risk Seth.

"Tougher than some pissant who has to hide behind a mob to make himself feel like a big strong man. What are you compensating for, buddy?" Ty's voice drawled the question lazily and Noah shook his head. You'd think a former Army Ranger would have more sense than to poke at the enemy with people's lives on the line, but Ty had never been what Noah would consider predictable.

"The only reason I haven't shot you in the head, you miserable sack of nothing, is that I'm waiting on one of your loved ones to show up so they can watch the life drain out of you. That might be avoidable if you tell me where the boy is."

Ty laughed and Noah nearly sagged with relief. They'd hidden Seth somehow. In the cellar maybe? It'd be impossible to get him out of there without Peter seeing him and Vanessa, if she was down there with him.

Noah winced as a flash of light hit his peripheral vision. He did a quick scan of the tree line, but he didn't see anyone or any sign of a gun. He turned his attention back to the cracked door of the cabin, but the flash of light persisted. *Flash. Flash. Flash.*

Noah studied the tree line, over and over again, seeing no sign of anyone. Another flash, and he finally got it.

It was coming from the barn, and since it seemed purposeful rather than the precursor to being picked off, Noah moved toward it.

He wouldn't lead Peter to Seth again, so he took a long circuitous way that involved using some of the other men's tracks to hopefully throw anyone off the scent, then his own back into the woods. Once hidden in the trees, he took off on a dead run.

When he reached the back of the barn, he gave three short raps against it. When they were returned in double time, he rounded the corner. He kept his body close to the barn, dragging his feet hoping to make the trail simply look like melted snow runoff causing a rut in the snow.

When he reached the barn opening, which had no closure anymore as the barn was almost never used and falling apart, he slid inside.

Vanessa was holding a very frightened-and bundled-up-looking Seth. She had a quilt around them that had hay stuck all over it, and he assumed Vanessa had hidden them in a pile of old hay.

Noah winced, but he didn't have time to worry about whether Seth was comfortable. He had to keep the boy alive. "What's going on?"

"We heard them coming. Ty sent me to the barn. I have no idea what's going on aside from that. I've been trying to stay hidden, but Ty's been in there so long…" She bit her lip, sending an uncharacteristic worried look toward the cabin.

"I heard him. He's holding his own, it appears. They've got men watching the road, but none watching the cabin. I don't think they expected to be followed, but maybe they're expecting police to show up. They think Addie's dead. She's in the secret passageway. I need you to go get her. She'll lead you to Annabelle, then you take the quickest route to Bent."

He started pulling Vanessa toward the opening, glancing every which way before he nodded toward the back of the cabin.

"What about you?" Vanessa asked as she ran.

"Ty and I will take care of it." He did his best to hurriedly cover the tracks they were making. "Get Addie and go. Now."

"If either of you die, I swear to God I'll find a way to make you pay," Vanessa said angrily, eyes suspiciously shiny.

"Love you, too, Van," Noah muttered, pulling the rifle off his back. "Now get him and her the hell out of here."

With one last angry look, she gave a nod and pulled the door open. Noah kept watch, ready to shoot anyone who might appear and try to intercept.

Addie scooted out, wide-eyed, and then immediately held out her arms and Seth fell into them, crying faintly. Addie soothed him, and Vanessa encouraged her into a run toward the trees.

She never even looked his way.

Chapter Seventeen

Addie wished she could go faster, but following the small marks on the tree back to Annabelle wasn't as easy as it had sounded an hour or so ago. Though she could somewhat follow the disturbance in the snow that was her and Noah's covered tracks from earlier, the wind and fading daylight had made that difficult as well.

Vanessa had a thin, weak flashlight out and Addie was using her fingers to feel the bark of the trees for the heavy slash of a cut. But Seth clung to her, whimpering unhappily, and that kept her going regardless of the frustration.

"It's okay, baby," she murmured, searching the trees, every pain and ache in her body fading to a dull numbness.

"Here's the next," Vanessa announced. They'd been trying to cover their tracks, at the very least obscure how many people had run away from the cabin. It was all getting so tiring, and she needed to get Seth somewhere warm, even if he was bundled to the hilt.

"Man, you guys sure made a trek," Vanessa mumbled as they searched the next grouping of trees.

"Noah wants them to think I'm dead."

In the dim twilight Vanessa looked back at her. "Dead? Well, that's smart. I'd prefer *him* dead, but that'd do, too."

"And Seth."

Vanessa's eyebrow winged up as she went back to searching the trees. "How's that going to work?"

"I don't know. I'm taking ideas." Addie sighed and stood to her full height. "Here's the next."

A huffing sound caught both women's attention and they looked toward it. Addie nearly cried from relief as Vanessa ran the few yards to Annabelle.

"There you are, sweetheart," Vanessa offered to the horse, running a hand over her mane. "I bet you're cold. Let's get you home, yeah?"

Addie approached as Vanessa pulled some feed out of the saddlebag and fed it to Annabelle by hand. Vanessa looked at her and Seth and then pressed her lips together.

"This is going to be tough and slow going. We're going to have to do this bareback so we all fit, and go slow so Seth is safe."

Addie swallowed at the lump in her throat. "Do you think we'll make it?"

"We won't know until we try. Once we get somewhere warm, we'll figure out a way to make it look like Seth's... Well."

Addie didn't like to say it, either, even if it was just a ruse they were planning. It felt too possible, too real, especially on the run from Peter.

"The dark is going to be a problem," Vanessa said flatly. "I could maneuver Bent blindfolded and turned around, but these forests and mountains? It's another story."

"Can't we make our way to the road?" Addie asked as Vanessa unbuckled the saddle and dropped it to the ground.

"Noah thinks Peter has men on the road. Any ideas on where to hide the saddle? If we're trying to hide the fact more than just me and Seth escaped, we can't leave this lying around."

"We'll bury it," Addie said resolutely.

"It'll take time."

"I think it's time we have." She had to hope it was time they had. As long as Peter wasn't after them, they had to do everything they could to hide the fact that she was still alive. "We could use it maybe. Make it look like the horse threw you and Seth and the saddle. A horrible, bloody accident. Then we see if Laurel can get someone at the hospital to forge records or something."

"Far-fetched. A horse couldn't throw a saddle, and that's only for starters."

"Peter wouldn't know that. He'd see a saddle and blood and then we'll leave the horse's prints and go straight for town. Get someone, anyone, to drive us to the hospital and see what we can fabricate from there."

Vanessa considered. "We'll need blood."

Addie shifted Seth onto her hip, then pulled the sheathed knife out of the back of her pants.

Vanessa swore under her breath. "You aren't really going to cut yourself open for this, are you?"

"Better me doing the cutting than Peter." Addie grimaced at the thought. "Well, you might have to do the cutting."

Vanessa swore again. "I don't know how you got into this mess, Addie, but boy do you owe me once we're through it."

"Then let's get through it." With that, Addie set about to create quite the fictional scene.

NOAH WANTED TO give Addie and Vanessa as much time as possible to get a head start before he engaged with Peter and his men, but the longer Ty stayed in there at the mercy of a mobster, the less chance his mouthy brother had of escaping unscathed.

When Noah had returned to the door after watching Vanessa, Addie and Seth disappear into the woods, it had been closed so there was no hope of overhearing more. Maybe he could sneak down the road and try to pick off Peter's men? Then there'd be no one to come running if he and Ty overpowered Peter.

But the problem remained: he couldn't see inside the cabin. He had no idea what weapons Peter had or what he might have already done to Ty.

And how much longer did he give Addie and Seth and Vanessa before he stepped in and helped his brother?

He frowned at a faint noise. Something like horse hooves off in the far distance. Couldn't be Addie and Vanessa, because the sound was more than one horse. Could they have reached help already?

Noah stayed where he was, scrunched into a little crevice in the outside logs of the cabin that gave him some cover. A horse came into view, but it wasn't anyone Noah recognized, which meant it had to be one of Peter's men.

How the hell did he get a horse? Noah seriously considered shooting the stranger, but he stopped himself. He didn't know what Peter was doing to Ty in that cabin, and he couldn't risk his brother's life.

The man dismounted stiffly if adeptly. Almost as though he'd been given rote instruction on horseback riding but hadn't had much practice. He went straight for the snowmobile, far too close to Noah for any kind of comfort.

But the man didn't look his direction. He tried to start the vehicle and was met with silence. He swore ripely, then pulled a walkie-talkie out of his coat pocket.

"Snowmobile's been tampered with," the man said flatly into the radio.

Static echoed through the yard and Noah tried to think of some way to incapacitate the man without making sound.

"Leave it. Search the woods on horseback. Someone has my kid and is trying to get to Bent. We can't let them." It was Peter's voice, Noah was fairly sure.

Noah didn't have time to worry anymore. He had to act. As silently as he could, he pulled his rifle out of the back case. He couldn't risk shooting the man and having anyone hear the gunshot, so he'd have to use it as a different kind of weapon.

He took a step out of his little alcove, and the man was too busy fiddling with the snowmobile to notice. Another step, holding his breath, slowly raising the rifle to be used as a bludgeon.

Without warning, the man whirled, his hand immediately going for the gun he wore on his side. Noah had been prepared for the sudden movement, though, and used the rifle to smack the gun out of the man's hand before he could raise it to shoot. Noah leaped forward and hit the butt of the weapon against the man's skull as hard as he could.

The man fell to his feet, groaning and grasping the ground—either for his own weapon or to push himself up, but Noah pressed his boot to the back of the man's neck. The man gurgled in pain.

Before Noah could think what to do next, the front door was flung open and Noah raised his rifle, finger on the trigger, a second away from shooting.

But Ty was the one who emerged, and immediately hit the deck upon seeing Noah's rifle.

"Help me out here," Noah ordered.

"Thought I was going to die at my own brother's hand," Ty muttered, and it was only as he struggled to get to his feet that Noah realized he was tied up.

"What the hell is going on?"

"Oh, that idiot burst in and I let him think he had the upper hand so Van could get the kid away. He tied me up. Yapped at me till I thought I was going to die of boredom, but he was searching the house the entire time."

"Where's he now?" Noah asked, pushing his boot harder against the squirming man's neck.

"He found the passageway," Ty muttered disgustedly. "Smarter than he seems. He's got radio contact with his men. Somehow they got horses. Can't imagine they know how to ride them, but the idea was to start searching the tree perimeter. He's got some fancy GPS and all sorts of crap. They're out there, looking for them."

"Get over here."

Ty complied. When the gasping man on the

ground grasped for his leg, Ty kicked him in the side.

Noah retrieved his Swiss Army knife, then used it to cut the zip ties that were keeping Ty's hands together and behind his back.

"Managed to get out of the ones around my feet, but the hands were a bit harder."

"Thought Army Rangers could escape anything."

"I'd have done it eventually. But I heard a commotion. Figured I didn't have much time. Luckily it was just you."

"And Peter is out there."

"Van'll keep Addie safe."

Noah glanced down at the man, who was still struggling weakly against his boot. "Addie's dead," Noah said flatly.

"What?" Ty demanded on an exhale.

Noah brought a finger to his lips, mimed being quiet, and his brother seemed to catch on. "Peter set a fire on the property. She died in it."

"Then he'll pay," Ty said, his voice nothing but acid, which Noah wasn't even sure was all for show.

"Yes, he will. Get me something to tie this garbage up with."

Ty nodded and disappeared back inside. He

returned with some cords. "These will have to do."

They worked together to tie the man's hands and legs together around an old flagpole in the front yard. He fought them, but weakly, and in just a few minutes he was tightly secured to the pole.

Noah moved to the back of the cabin, searching the perimeter for any signs of Peter or his men. Peter had left tracks from the back of the cabin to the trees, so that was something.

"We're outnumbered," Ty said from behind Noah. He slid the other man's gun into his coat pocket. "We've got one horse and no vehicle. How are we going to catch this guy?"

Noah looked around at the trees and the mountains as shadowy sentries in the dark. The moon shone above, bright and promising. The night was frigid, but he and Ty had survived worse. "Wyoming is how we're going to catch this guy."

Chapter Eighteen

Addie's arm burned where she'd had Vanessa cut it. Without warning or discussion, Vanessa had subsequently made a rather nasty-looking cut on her own arm.

"Sure hope we can get a tetanus shot or something at the hospital," Vanessa had muttered before grabbing a handful of snow and mixing it with the blood.

Seth was pretending to ride the saddle that they'd placed in the snow as Addie and Vanessa worked to make two arm cuts look like enough blood to have been blunt force trauma to the head. Once they'd done as much as they could and were teeth-shatteringly cold, they bandaged each other up with the first aid kit that had been in Annabelle's pack.

Addie shot Seth worried glances as they did all this, because despite the layers he was wearing, the snow would make him wet and it was nightfall. The temperature had been dropping steadily, seemingly every minute.

Vanessa used her weakened flashlight to survey their supposed accident scene. It didn't look nearly as gruesome as Addie had hoped, even in the mix of silvery moonlight filtering through the trees and faded yellow glow of a too-small flashlight. "How will they even see it?"

"I imagine they're a little better equipped than we are. High-powered flashlights, headlights if they can get that snowmobile out here. Besides, they might not even be after us yet. Maybe they won't start looking till daylight."

"True." But if that was the case, they might not see it at all, and all this work for nothing. She shook her head. She couldn't think like that. As long as they got to safety without Peter knowing she was alive, they'd succeeded. The rest of the plan could still work.

She scooped Seth off the saddle, much to his dismay. He began to kick and scream. "He needs food. A diaper change."

Vanessa nodded, then moved the faint glow of her flashlight to Annabelle. "Let's get going, then. I think we've done the best we can."

It was some doing getting back on the horse without a saddle and getting Seth situated between them, but eventually they were on their way. Seth fussed and fidgeted, small mewling cries in the middle of a dark forest.

But moonlight led their way, and Addie focused on the hope. She didn't allow herself to consider if Noah and Ty were okay, if Peter knew what was going on. She didn't think about the future any further than them reaching Bent without problem.

Seth was beginning to doze, something about the rocking motion of the horse soothing him enough to be taken over by sleep. Addie was feeling a little droopy herself, but holding on to Vanessa and Seth between them kept her from nodding off.

Addie wasn't sure how long they trotted through the freezing cold night. The wind was frigid and rattled the trees. The moon shone high and bright and yet gave off no warmth and very little hope.

Seth finally went totally limp in her arms, asleep despite all the danger around them—from people and from the elements. Every once in a while Addie thought it'd be simpler to just lie in the snow and sleep. She was so tired—exhausted physically, tired of fighting a man who'd never give up.

Then Vanessa slowed the horse on a quiet murmur.

"Are we there?"

Vanessa shook her head. "I hear something," she said quietly. Moonlight glinted her dark hair silver, but the dark shrouded her face so Addie couldn't read her expression.

Then Addie heard it, too, and they both winced as a beam of light glanced over the trees. Faint, far in the distance, but coming for them.

"Maybe it's Noah," Addie whispered.

"Not with that kind of light."

Which Addie knew, but she'd just wanted something to hope for. But what would false hope get her? Dead probably. All of them dead. "Let me off. Take Seth. I'll create a diversion."

"No."

"It's the only way. They'll catch us, and I can't let Peter ever get his hands on Seth. I just can't."

"He's supposed to think you're dead."

"Then it'll be even more of a diversion when I'm not. I can't control the horse, Vanessa, and even if I could you have a much better chance of finding Bent than I do. Let me off. I'll scream bloody murder while you ride fast as you can to town."

"They'll kill you, Addie."

"Maybe." She'd made her peace with that in the burning building. She would die for Seth. She had to be willing. "Seth is the most important thing. That was an agreement Noah and I made when we came back here. Peter doesn't care much whether I live or die. I'm a game for him, but he does want Seth or at least convinced himself he does if only to punish me. So we do everything not to give him what he wants. I'll scream—you ride toward town. I'll lead them back to our little scene saying Seth is dead. If I don't make it, I trust you Carsons will make sure Seth is safe."

"Addie…"

But she could tell Vanessa was relenting, so she shifted Seth until she could push him forward into Vanessa's lap. Seth began to whimper and Addie awkwardly slid off the horse. "There's no time. They can't hear him crying. Go. Fast. As fast as you can."

"Cut the little bastard open with that knife of yours. Do whatever you have to do to stay alive. I'll send all the help here the minute I get to town."

"Just go," Addie said. "Keep my baby safe."

Vanessa hesitated. "I'm going to keep Annabelle walking slow and quiet until I hear you scream. Then we'll gallop. Scream as loud and long as you can and hopefully they won't hear me. If you see any split off and come after me, scream 'bear.' It might be enough of a distraction to give me a leg up."

"Okay," Addie agreed. The thought of one of Peter's men breaking off and going after Vanessa scared her to her bones, but splitting up was the best way. The only way. She'd wail and scream and pretend Seth was already dead and pray to God it didn't turn out to be true.

Vanessa urged Annabelle into motion, a quiet walk the opposite direction of the murmuring noise and moving lights. They were definitely closer, but a ways off.

Addie started to walk toward them. Her heart beat hard in her chest, and fear and cold made it hard to move through the snow, but she marched forward. Closer and closer until the swath of light started to hit her.

Then she began to scream.

NOAH WAS TIRED of the wound on his side holding him back, and yet he couldn't seem to push himself or the horse beneath them harder than he already was. He had no idea where Peter's man had gotten this horse, but it wasn't as adept as his horses back at the ranch.

The snow was deep and the air frigid cold, and while he'd been used to cold his whole life, something about the fear of losing the people he loved made it heavier, harder.

Or was that the gunshot wound to his side that he may or may not have accidentally ripped the stitches out of?

He didn't mention that to Ty. He didn't mention anything to Ty as they rode on, following the trail of Peter's men.

"Don't know where this horse came from, but it's not used to this kind of weather or terrain," Ty said grimly.

"Maybe not, but we've covered more ground than we would've on foot." Noah surveyed the tracks in front of them. Peter's tracks converged with two pairs of horse's tracks not too far from the cabin. They'd been following the horse tracks back down toward the road, but then the tracks abruptly turned back into the trees toward the mountains.

"You think these idiots have any idea what they're doing?" Ty asked disgustedly.

"Doesn't look like it. Doesn't mean they're not dangerous."

"True enough."

Out of nowhere, causing both Noah and Ty to flinch in surprise, a bloodcurdling scream ripped through the night.

They didn't even exchange a glance before they leaned forward in tandem on the horse, urging it to move toward the scream as fast as it could. The horse might not have been experienced or used to the terrain, but it seemed to understand panic.

There was moonlight, but far in the distance an unnatural light moving around as well. And the scream. It just kept going, with only minimal pauses for the screamer to breathe.

He tried not to think about who the screamer was, though there were only two possibilities, and he knew it wasn't Vanessa. But he couldn't allow himself to ponder what Addie might be screaming about, or why.

He only had to get to her. To the screaming, whoever it might be and for whatever reason.

"Stop," Noah ordered abruptly.

"What?" Ty demanded, but he brought the horse to a stop.

"I'll go on foot and sneak around the opposite direction. They have more men, more weapons. We need the element of surprise."

"Agreed, but I should be the one on foot. You're favoring that side, brother."

"I'll live."

"You keep saying that."

"And it'll keep being true." Noah dismounted without letting Ty argue further. "You go straight for the lights, slow and quiet. I'll circle around. I promised Addie we'd keep that baby safe, so he's our first priority. We don't risk him, and you don't risk you."

"But you can risk you, I'm assuming."

"I won't do anything stupid." But if he had to make some sacrifices, then so be it. "Go."

Ty nodded grimly in the moonlight, and Noah took off in a dead sprint. He circled the light instead of going for it, using the moonlight as his guide and the trees as his protection.

Everything in his body burned. His wound, his lungs, his eyes. Still, he pushed forward, adrenaline rushing through him.

He was finally close enough to see people,

so he slowed his pace, hid behind a tree and watched the morbid procession of shadows.

Between moonlight and their flashlights, he could make out the odd scene moving toward him. He tried to make sense of what he was seeing. Peter was pushing Addie through the snow, while two men on horseback followed with their guns pointed at her. But they were *following* her, and she was leading them somewhere most definitely not in the direction of the cabin or Bent.

Where was Vanessa? Seth? Had Addie sacrificed herself? Had they escaped undetected? Or had something horrible happened?

Addie slowed, stumbled, and fell to her hands and knees in the snow.

"Get up," Peter ordered. "Or I'll really give you a reason to fall."

Addie struggled to her feet and it took everything in Noah not to jump forward and gather her up in the safety of his arms. But that would only get them both killed.

Still, he and Ty had the element of surprise. They could take out three guys, if they were careful. If they were smart.

"Move!" Peter ordered in a booming yell.

"I'm lost. I don't know where..."

"You better figure it out because if you

don't show me the boy's dead body, I'm going to think you're lying, Addie. Then you'll be dead and I'll make sure that boy has the most hellish life you could ever imagine."

"He's your son. He's dead. Don't you have any compassion?"

Dead. Seth, dead. Addie wouldn't be walking let alone coherent if that were true, so it was all part of the plan. To make Peter think Seth was dead, but why hadn't Addie stayed out of it so Peter could think she was dead as well?

"You stole from me, Addie. You lied to me. You caused the death of my son and you dare speak to me of compassion? I should kill you right here and find the boy's body myself, if you're even telling the truth."

Addie stopped her stumbling forward and turned to face him. "Fine, Peter. Kill me."

Noah was so shocked he didn't breathe, and apparently the words shocked Peter as well since he didn't say anything or raise his weapon.

"Do you think I won't?"

"I know you're capable," Addie said. "You killed my sister. She wouldn't run, I realize now. That's why you killed her. I don't know how many other people you've killed, and you've made me into a killer as well. I've been running from you for nearly a year and now here we are and what's the *point*? I'll never have a normal life. You'll always be a black cloud over it, so kill me."

"You will not dictate when or how I kill you."

"I guess we'll see."

Peter raised his hand, presumably to hit Addie, and Noah didn't think, didn't plan, he barely even aimed. He simply raised his gun and shot.

Peter howled in pain, but didn't go down. *Damn it*. His men were already heading toward Noah, so he had to run, rifle in hand.

They were on horseback, so Noah zigzagged through trees, then pivoted suddenly and cut back in the opposite direction. He heard them swear.

"Get off your horse and run!" one of the men yelled at the other.

Noah tried to use the head start to his advantage, but when he circled back neither Addie nor Peter were to be seen. He tried to search the area for tracks, make sense of any of them, but there was a man coming for him and…

A gunshot rang out and Noah dove to the

ground. The tree next to him exploded and Noah could only army-crawl through the snow trying to find a cluster of evergreens he could hide from the moonlight in.

"I can't see a damn thing!" one of the men yelled. "Get over here with the light."

Noah heard the horse hooves even over the heavy beating of his heart. He had to get to Addie before these men caught him, but where on earth had she and Peter disappeared to?

Another gunshot, this one even closer, the beating of horse hooves and the shining light of whatever high-powered flashlight they had flashing across him.

But that would give him everything he needed. He zigzagged through trees for a few more minutes before finding a large trunk to settle behind. He pulled the rifle off his back, watched the light move, and then shot.

When the light shook and fell, Noah knew he'd hit his target. But that was only one of the men. He needed to find the one who'd been on the horse. Noah searched the woods for signs of another flashlight beam, but found nothing.

Then, faintly, he heard grunts and followed the sound, finding Ty grappling on the ground with someone next to a prancing horse.

When the man who was decidedly not Ty pulled out a knife that glinted in the moonlight, Noah saw red. He lunged at the man on top of his brother, rolling him onto his stomach and shoving his knee into the man's back as he pulled his arms back. The man screamed in pain, as Noah wasn't very gentle or worried about the natural ways a man's arm should go. The guy's entire body went limp.

Noah didn't believe it at first, but as he eased off the man he didn't move. He glanced over at Ty, who was struggling to get into a sitting position.

"Stabbed me right in the arm," Ty rasped, and Noah winced as Ty easily pulled a large, daggerlike knife out of where it had been lodged in his biceps.

Noah got to his feet, aches and pains and injuries nothing but a dull ache as fear overtook his body. "He's got Addie."

"Go. I'll bandage myself up and get to you soon as I can."

Noah nodded. "You die, you'll be sorry."

Ty smiled thinly in the moonlight. "I've been through a lot worse. This'll be the last thing that does me in. Now go."

So Noah did.

Chapter Nineteen

Peter pushed her until she fell. Again and again and again. She would lie there in the freezing cold until he kicked her, demanding she get to her feet.

"Get up," Peter demanded, kicking her. She wanted to kick him back. Fight him with everything she had, with everything she was, but *time* was the most important thing. Not revenge. Not yet.

"What for?" Maybe she was going a little over the top, but the more Peter believed she wanted to die, the more her lie that Seth was dead held weight. What was there to live for if Seth was dead?

He kicked her harder, enough she cried out. "Get up and show me his body and then maybe I'll put you out of your misery."

"You don't need me to find him."

When he kicked her again, Addie got to her

feet. She didn't have to fake her shivering or her exhaustion. She didn't have to fake her fear or her sadness, because she had no idea who'd fired that shot at Peter. She had no idea if Vanessa had gotten Seth to safety.

She knew nothing. So all she could do was move forward with the determination this would end. Seth would be safe and this would be *over*, once and for all.

Addie had lost track of where she was in the dark forest, but the longer she and Peter walked in circles, the longer Vanessa had to get safe.

When a gunshot echoed from far away, Addie jerked in its direction. Between the moon and Peter's flashlight, his face was a ghostly silver white as he smiled.

"I don't suppose you think whoever failed at saving you just got shot by one of my men."

"Or whoever shot at you shot at them."

He gave her another hard shove so she fell in yet another icy pile of snow. His gun flashed. "Maybe I will just kill you, worthless as you are."

Addie hesitated a moment, not sure if she should goad him into continuing to believe she had a death wish when she most certainly did not. She couldn't find words as

Peter slowly pressed the barrel of the gun to her temple.

Addie swallowed, trying to rein in the shaking of her body. "I'll beg," she offered, her voice a raspy whisper. "I'll get on my knees and beg you to put a bullet through my head." Because it would add time. Everything that added time had to be good.

And if he took her up on it, well…

Peter leaned in close, his lips touching her ear as he spoke. She shuddered in disgust as he whispered. "I want you to *suffer*, Addie. I couldn't take time with your sister, but I'll take my time with you. Now, admit you're lying or show me the boy's body in the next ten minutes, or I'll start breaking fingers for every extra minute I'm out here in this godforsaken wasteland."

Her patience was fraying and she opened her mouth to tell him to go jump off a cliff, but managed to swallow the words down before she really did get herself killed. If only because he'd mentioned her sister. Seth's mother, who'd died for no other reason than she'd fallen for the wrong kind of man.

Addie turned away from Peter, trying to study her surroundings, trying to figure out where she needed to go. If she led him to the scene she and Vanessa had created, there'd be no body, but maybe she could convince Peter bears or wolves or some Wild West–sounding animal got there first.

She looked up at the moon and tried to use it as a guide. Where had it been when they'd gotten on Annabelle? Could you navigate via the moon? Someone probably could, but she wasn't so certain *she* could.

Still, she moved. Because it ate up time. Time was the important thing right now. Not her life. Not the moon. Not Noah or the future. Just time.

"Stop," Peter hissed, yanking her by Noah's coat. Peter spanned the flashlight over the trees around them in a circle.

"What is it? Do you think it's a bear?"

He shoved her to the ground and she landed hard on her hands.

"It's not a bear, you idiot."

"Wolf?" she asked weakly.

He shone the light directly in her eyes and she winced away.

"Are there wolves?" Peter demanded.

"Yes. Yes. They're nocturnal. Wolves are. A-and here." She thought, maybe. Noah had definitely mentioned coyotes, but wolves sounded a lot more terrifying, and what did it matter if she was wrong? She wanted Peter to be scared. That was all that mattered.

Again Peter slowly moved the beam of light around in a circle. Addie stayed where she was in the snow praying there was no wolf or bear or anything. Just Noah. She prayed and prayed for Noah.

Peter raised his gun and shot. Addie screamed and covered her ears as he turned in a slow circle, pulling the trigger every few seconds.

"What kind of coward hides in the shadows?" Peter demanded. "A man shows his face when he's ready to fight."

"A man doesn't chase an innocent woman and her child across the country, terrorize her and cause the death of his men because of his own stupidity."

Noah. It was Noah's voice in the woods. Peter shot toward the voice, and Addie swallowed back a gasp. Her ears rang with the sound of all the gunshots and she wanted to go running for him. Save him. Hold him.

"*Her* child? Is that what she told you?" Peter laughed. Uproariously. "That boy is *mine*. She has no claim on him."

Silence stretched in the freezing dark, and Addie wanted to cry, but she couldn't allow herself. It didn't matter. If Noah was angry or hurt, or if he believed Peter at all. Nothing in the here and now mattered except Seth's safety, and Noah's getting out of here alive. He shouldn't die for the problems she'd brought to his door.

So if he was hurt that she'd lied about being Seth's mother, it didn't matter. Couldn't.

"What a little liar you are," Peter said cheerfully. "Your big strong man thought you were a doting mother? How adorable."

"I am his aunt," Addie returned. "And his protector."

"If he's dead, you failed."

"I suppose I did fail, but better him dead than with you where you'd only warp and twist him into a sad, pathetic excuse for a human being. Better him gone for good than turn out to be anything like you."

Without warning, Peter snatched an arm out and curled his hand around her throat. The flashlight thumped to the ground, bouncing light against the snow. Addie tried to fight him, kick at him, but he'd holstered his gun and added his other hand around her throat. He was too strong or she was too cold.

"I'm going to choke her to death," Peter called out. "Are you going to just stand there and watch?"

There were only the gurgling sounds coming from her own throat as she clawed at his hands. He'd wanted her to suffer, but now he wanted Noah to suffer by watching him kill her. What was Noah doing? Why wasn't he stepping in to save her?

She began to see spots, everything in her body screaming in agony. She considered how much of a chance she had at running if she stabbed Peter. Panic rose like bile in her throat and she no longer cared what the consequences were. If she failed, she failed, but at least she'd tried not to die.

She kept clawing at him with one hand, but with the other she reached behind her and pulled the knife in her pants out of its sheath. Peter was too busy searching the dark for Noah, so she swung the blade as hard as she could. It hit Peter's side with a sickening squelch and for a moment she could pull in a gasping breath as his hands eased around her throat.

But then she saw Peter's eyes widen, then narrow, and everything inside her sank. The squeezing returned as his lip curled into a sneer.

She hadn't gotten the blade far enough inside him to cause any kind of damage. And now, since Noah was apparently not coming to save her, she was dead.

As long as Seth's safe. As long as Seth's safe. She let her mind chant it as her vision dimmed again.

"You stupid girl. You think that little knife would—" But Peter never finished his sentence, because the sound of a gun going off seemed simultaneous to him falling to the ground.

FOR A SECOND or two, Noah could only stand where he'd positioned himself behind a tree, rifle still up. But Addie was standing there, next to Peter's unmoving body. Then she collapsed onto her knees, making terrible gasping noises, but gasping noises were alive noises.

Noah's whole body shook as he rushed forward. Peter's body didn't so much as move. Noah didn't bother to look where his bullet had hit. He gathered Addie up in his arms and began to carry her away. He wanted her far away from that man, the ugliness, the violence.

He carried her through the trees, struggling against the exhaustion, his body's own injuries, the cold. But still he moved forward, back toward where he'd left Ty. But his legs only kept him upright for so long.

"I can walk. I can walk," she murmured against his neck as he leaned against a tree, trying to catch his breath. "We can walk, right? If you got away from the other guys, they're… Do you think they're all dead?"

"I don't know about dead, but you're right, we can walk." He set her down carefully, still leaning against the tree, trying to catch his breath and wrap his mind around all of it.

"Seth's alive, isn't he?" Because that was the most important thing, what this had all been for.

"I think so. I told Vanessa to go with him. We were trying…" She choked on a sob, and it hurt to look at her, even in the shadowy light of night. She was pale and bloodied and dripping wet.

"We need to move. Make sure they're safe. I have to find Ty, and then…" He looked around the forest, the starry moonlit sky above. "We'll get to Seth," he promised, holding out his hand for her to take. But when she slipped her hand into his, he had to pull her close again and hold her tight against him for a minute. Just a minute.

"What's a little hypothermia, right?" she

asked, her arms around him nearly as tight as his were around her.

He managed a chuckle against her hair, holding her close to assure himself she was alive and well. This was over. *Over.* "We'll survive it, I think. Let's find Ty. He earned himself a little stab wound in the arm."

"So tetanus shots for everyone."

"All these near-death experiences turned you into quite the comedian."

"Or I've just gone insane." She sighed gustily into his neck. "Noah."

She didn't say anything more, so he held her to him, trying to will the cold away. "You're safe now. It's all over."

She sighed heavily. "Not all. Noah, Peter wasn't lying. Seth isn't mine."

"Maybe if you hadn't just almost died I'd care a little bit more about that." But mostly, Noah found he didn't care. Maybe before this had all gone down he would have mustered some righteous indignation, some *hurt*, but after seeing what Peter could do, there was no question everything Addie had done had been done to protect Seth from that monster.

He couldn't hold that against her.

She pulled back, looked up at him, and he

couldn't read her expression in the shadows. "I lied to you."

"Yeah. Yeah, well. Maybe Seth isn't your biological son, but he's in your care. He's your blood. To him, and to you I imagine, you're mother and child. A lie to keep Seth safe doesn't hurt me, and I know this whole time all you've been trying to do is keep Seth safe. I won't hold that against you or fault you for that, and no one can make me. Even you."

She expelled a breath. "Noah, I want to go home. I want Seth and I want to go home."

"Then that's what we'll do. Because this is over. You're safe, and once we know Seth's safe, that's all that will matter." Ever.

Chapter Twenty

The next few days were nothing but a blur. A hospital stay for her due to hypothermia and pneumonia, a hospital stay for Noah and Ty for their respective wounds. Vanessa and Seth were relatively unharmed, and to Addie, that was all that mattered.

The police and the FBI were a constant presence, talks of being a witness and trials. If charges would be pressed against her or Noah for killing men. Addie was almost grateful for being sick and not quite with it.

She was continually grateful for Laurel's presence and help. For Vanessa's bringing Seth to visit whenever the nurses would let her. Carsons and Delaneys working together to help someone who didn't really belong.

Bent is your home. Noah's voice echoed in her head. Bent was her home. But what did that mean? The Carson Ranch? This town?

He'd said he loved her once, and she hadn't had the opportunity to say it back.

Addie sat in the passenger seat of Laurel's car, Seth's car seat fastened in the back. Over three months ago, she'd made this exact trek. She hadn't had a clue what would befall her back then.

She didn't have a clue what would befall her now. Noah had been released this morning, and he hadn't come to see her.

"Maybe he doesn't want…" Addie cleared her throat as Laurel turned the car onto the gravel road that led up to the Carson Ranch. "He might not want me here. I did lie to him." He'd said it didn't matter, but that was in the aftermath of hell. Now it might matter.

"He wants you here," Laurel replied. "I am under strict orders."

Addie slid Laurel a look. "From who?"

Laurel smiled. "Too many Carsons to count."

"I don't want to… I brought all these terrible things on him, and he didn't even come see me in the hospital. Why would he want me here?"

"I think that's something you'll have to ask the man yourself. I also think you already know the answer to that, so you might not want to insult him and ask him that in quite those words."

"He could've died. A million times."

"So could you. And Seth. But somehow, you all fought evil together and won. I'd pat myself on the back, not worry about if Noah is overly offended by the sacrifices he willingly made." Laurel frowned. "I am sorry we didn't—couldn't—do more. The police, me personally."

"Peter learned how to outmaneuver the police from birth, I think. I don't blame you, Laurel. We all did everything we could, and like you said, we all fought evil together and won."

"I suppose." Laurel smiled thinly. "And when you fight evil and win, then you face the rest of your life."

Addie blew out a breath and watched the house get closer and closer to view. "It feels like I've been running forever," she murmured, more to herself than to Laurel.

But Laurel responded anyway. "And now it's time to stop. There isn't anything or anyone to run from anymore, and if there ever is again, you have a whole town—Carsons *and* Delaneys—at your side." She stopped the car in front of the house.

Much like that first day all those months ago, Grady stepped out, his smile all for Laurel. Addie stayed in her seat, waiting for some sign, some *hint* that Noah actually wanted her here. She might have believed it in the snow and the woods at night, but in the light of hospital days and FBI questions, all her fears and worries repopulated and grew.

He'd kept his distance. He was spending his days talking to FBI agents because of her. Maybe it'd had to be done, but that didn't make it any less her fault. She'd lied to him. Maybe once he really thought about it, he'd realized he didn't love a liar.

Laurel had gotten out and was pulling Seth out of his car seat. Grady was unlatching the car seat from Laurel's car. And still Addie sat, staring at the house, wondering what a future of freedom really looked like.

Freedom. No longer a slave to whether or not Peter would find her. She was *free*. Sitting in front of the Carson ranch house, it was the first time that fact truly struck her.

She stepped out of the car. Laurel handed Seth to her and he wiggled and squirmed, pointing at the house, then clapping delightedly. "No!"

"Yes, we're home with Noah, aren't we?"

Because she was free now. Free to take what she wanted, have it, nurture it. Free to do what was best for Seth's well-being, not just his safety. Free to build a life.

A real life.

If Noah was mad at her for bringing Peter to his doorstep, mad at her for lying about Seth not being her biological child, well, she'd find a way to make up for it. She'd find a way to make his words true.

Bent is your home.

I love you.

Grady took the car seat to the front door and Laurel placed the bag she'd brought to the hospital with some of Addie's things next to it.

"We're going to head out," Grady said.

"You aren't coming in?"

"Uh, no. You enjoy your homecoming."

"My…" She glanced at the door. *Home-coming.*

"Call if you need anything, or if the FBI get too obnoxious," Laurel offered, walking back to her car hand in hand with Grady.

Then it was just her and Seth, standing on the porch of the Carson Ranch, alone. It felt like a new start somehow.

And it was. A new start. Freedom. A life to build. But she had to take that step forward.

She had to let go of the fear…not just of what her life had been, but of what she'd allowed herself to be. A victim of fear and someone else's power.

Never again.

She took a deep breath, steeling herself to barge in and demand Noah have a heart-to-heart conversation with her. No grunts. No silences. No *I love yous* and then disappearances. They weren't on the run anymore and he couldn't—

The door swung open.

"Well, are you going to come in or are you just planning on standing out in the cold all day?" Noah asked gruffly.

She blinked up at his tall, broad form filling up the doorframe. "I thought I'd stare at the door for a bit longer."

"I see you're still being funny."

"No!" Seth lunged for Noah and Noah caught him easily.

"There's a boy," Noah murmured, the smile evident even beneath the beard. His gaze moved up to Addie, that smile still in place as he held Seth and Seth immediately grabbed for his hat hanging off the hook next to them.

"Come inside, Addie."

Right. Come inside. Conversation. She'd

tell him what she wanted. What she needed, and…and…

She stepped inside and Noah closed the door behind her.

"How are you feeling?"

"How am I feeling?" she repeated, staring at him, something like anger simmering inside her. She didn't know why, and it was probably unearned anger, but it was there nonetheless. "That's all you have to say to me?"

"No."

She frowned at him. "You don't make any sense."

"You were just released from the hospital," he said, as if that explained anything.

"So were you!"

"I wasn't sick, though."

"Oh, no, just a gunshot wound."

It was his turn to frown. "Why are we fighting exactly?"

Addie turned away from him. She didn't know why she was arguing or what she felt or…

She stopped abruptly in the middle of the living room when she saw a sign hanging from the exposed beams of the kitchen ceiling. Hand-painted and not quite neat, two simple words were written across the paper.

Welcome Home.

He'd made her a sign. Hung it up. Home. *Home.* She turned back to face him, and all the tears she'd been fighting so hard for the past few days let loose in a torrent of relief.

"But… I lied to you. I made your life a living hell for days, and through the beginning and the end I lied to you about Seth. You've had time to think about that now. Really think about it. You have to be sure—"

"I can't say I *like* being lied to, but I understand it. You were protecting Seth, and there's nothing about *that* I don't understand. But…"

Oh, God, there was a but. She nearly sank to her knees.

"We have to promise each other, both of us, no more lies. Even righteous ones. Because the only way we fought Peter was together. The only way we survived was together. There can't be any more lies or doing things on our own. We're in this together. Partners."

"Partners," she repeated, Seth still happily playing with the cowboy hat as Noah held him on his hip.

"No lies. No keeping things from each

other. We work together. Always. I promise you that, if you can promise me the same."

Addie swallowed, looking at this good man in front of her, holding a boy who wasn't biologically her son but was *hers* nonetheless. "I promise you that, Noah. With all of my heart I promise you that." She glanced up at the sign he'd made, this stoic, uncelebratory man. "I do want this to be my home," she whispered.

"Then it's yours," Noah returned, reaching out and wiping some of the tears from her cheeks.

"I love you, Noah."

There was *no* doubt under all that hair and Carson cowboy gruffness, Noah smiled, and when his mouth met hers, Addie knew she'd somehow found what she'd always been looking for, even in those days of running away.

Home. Love. A place to belong. A place to raise Seth, and a man who'd be the best role model for him.

"I hear there's some curse about Carsons and Delaneys," she murmured against his mouth.

"I don't believe in curses, Addie. I believe in us. Hell, we defeated the mob. What's a curse?"

"I'd say neither has anything on love."

"Or coming home. Where you belong."

Yes, Addie Foster belonged in Bent, Wyoming, on the Carson Ranch, with Noah Carson at her side, to love and be loved in return for as long as she breathed.

And nothing would ever change that.

* * * * *

Get 4 FREE REWARDS!

We'll send you 2 FREE Books plus 2 FREE Mystery Gifts.

Harlequin® Romantic Suspense books feature heart-racing sensuality and the promise of a sweeping romance set against the backdrop of suspense.

FREE
Value Over
$20

Get 4 FREE REWARDS!

We'll send you 2 FREE Books
<u>plus</u> 2 FREE Mystery Gifts.

Harlequin Presents® books feature a sensational and sophisticated world of international romance where sinfully tempting heroes ignite passion.

FREE
Value Over
$20

Get 4 FREE REWARDS!

We'll send you 2 FREE Books plus 2 FREE Mystery Gifts.

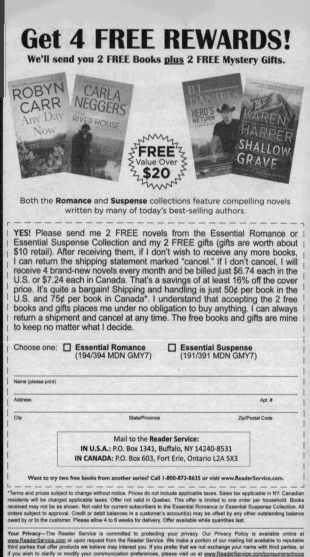

FREE Value Over **$20**

Both the **Romance** and **Suspense** collections feature compelling novels written by many of today's best-selling authors.

YES! Please send me 2 FREE novels from the Essential Romance or Essential Suspense Collection and my 2 FREE gifts (gifts are worth about $10 retail). After receiving them, if I don't wish to receive any more books, I can return the shipping statement marked "cancel." If I don't cancel, I will receive 4 brand-new novels every month and be billed just $6.74 each in the U.S. or $7.24 each in Canada. That's a savings of at least 16% off the cover price. It's quite a bargain! Shipping and handling is just 50¢ per book in the U.S. and 75¢ per book in Canada*. I understand that accepting the 2 free books and gifts places me under no obligation to buy anything. I can always return a shipment and cancel at any time. The free books and gifts are mine to keep no matter what I decide.

Choose one: ☐ **Essential Romance** (194/394 MDN GMY7) ☐ **Essential Suspense** (191/391 MDN GMY7)

Name (please print)

Address   Apt. #

City   State/Province   Zip/Postal Code

Mail to the **Reader Service:**
IN U.S.A.: P.O. Box 1341, Buffalo, NY 14240-8531
IN CANADA: P.O. Box 603, Fort Erie, Ontario L2A 5X3

Want to try two free books from another series? Call 1-800-873-8635 or visit www.ReaderService.com.

READERSERVICE.COM

Manage your account online!

- Review your order history
- Manage your payments
- Update your address

> ### *We've designed the Reader Service website just for you.*

Enjoy all the features!

- Discover new series available to you, and read excerpts from any series.
- Respond to mailings and special monthly offers.
- Browse the Bonus Bucks catalog and online-only exculsives.
- Share your feedback.